Emily and the
Green Circle

Emily and the Green Circle

by **MARY KENNEDY**

illustrated by
JODY A. LEE

SCHOLASTIC INC.

New York   Toronto   London   Auckland   Sydney

For Eva Moore, my superb editor,
and Joan Kennedy Taylor, my generous daughter,
who both helped Emily find
the Green Circle

ISBN 0-590-40656-6

12 11 10 9 8 7 6 5 4 3 2 1   7 8 9/8 0 1 2/9

Printed in the U.S.A.   28

First Scholastic printing, July 1987

Contents

1
Nine Miles from Nowhere

Emily's father was driving the motor home. Emily was in the seat next to him, staring out into the darkness, watching the road unwind before them while her mother slept on a bed in the back.

Emily's father was looking for a trailer camp where they could park for the night, but he had taken a wrong turn hours before, and they were lost on back roads. He had no idea where they were, nor even where they were headed.

Emily loved the night and the look of mysterious and shadowy trees in the Florida swamps on either side. After many miles of these tall cypresses, there were tangled jungles of many kinds of growth, then pine timber. Fields began to appear and an occasional farmhouse and the blurred shapes of resting cattle. There was a faint light over the earth as though the moon were on its way. They saw orange groves, bouquets of blackness in orderly rows.

They came to a sleeping village.

"I thought I'd never see a civilized community again!" Emily's father said.

The village had a pleasant look. There was a small church on one side and a few low buildings. Opposite, across the street, there was a row of shops built under an arcade in Spanish style. There was an air of age and even elegance. The street-lamps were wrought-iron lanterns and cast a dim light.

Emily's father pulled up under one of the streetlamps and unfolded a map. "Hold the flash-light for me, Emily," he said.

Emily was afraid that her mother would wake up and tell her to go to bed.

Her mother woke up. "Emily," she said sleepily, "it is very late. Go to bed."

"I can't right now, Mother," Emily said. "I have to help Father. I'm all ready for bed. I've had my shower, brushed my hair, cleaned my teeth, and I'm in my pajamas."

"There ought to be a shortcut to the ocean somewhere here," Emily's father murmured.

He started the engine and drove on a mile or so, then turned onto an unpaved road at the left. He went slowly. The headlights showed hedges and fenced land along a little-traveled road. Now and then there were glimpses of well-cared-for houses and gardens.

Suddenly the motor gave a sputter and stopped. Emily's father shifted gears and turned the key. The motor whirred loudly for a few seconds and finally sputtered back to life.

"What's the trouble?" asked Emily's mother.

"Something's wrong with the engine. Did either of you see a garage in the place we just passed? The gas is low, too."

"No," said Emily.

"It's too late anyway," said her mother. "What time is it?"

Emily's father looked at the clock on the dashboard. "About eleven-thirty," he said.

"You must go to bed, Emily. You've had a very long day and all that sightseeing yesterday in St. Augustine."

"I'm not tired," said Emily. Three days ago she had had her ninth birthday, and she felt that now she was old enough to stay up late once in a while. She hoped her father would be on her side, and she looked at him for support. Her father smiled at her. He thought Emily was a perfect child, and he almost never said no to anything she asked.

He looked again at the map and shook his head. "I've made a mistake. This place isn't on the map. It's about nine miles since we came to those crossroads. I'd better pull up somewhere before the engine dies completely." He drove along cautiously.

Emily's mother put on a robe and came to stand behind them.

"There's someone following us," she said.

"Nonsense," said her husband. "Why would anyone want to do that?"

But when he glanced in the side mirror, he saw the lights of a car not ten feet behind them.

"What can he want? It's a mighty lonely road," Emily's mother said.

Emily's father drew closer to the side of the road to give the other car room to pass, but the driver stayed right where he was behind them.

Emily rushed to the back window. "He's practically on our heels. It's a man with a pointed beard."

"The little I can see of him, he looks all right," her father said, "just a respectable citizen."

Emily's mother shivered and drew her robe closer. "Why doesn't he pass us?"

"He probably just wants to ask a question. He may be lost, too. Why don't I stop and ask him?"

"Don't you dare! That's all he needs. Besides, if he is lost, so are we. We couldn't help. Can't you go any faster, Edward?"

"I'll try, but it's risky. Don't be nervous, Elvira. It's not like you."

"I'm not really," Emily's mother said. "I just think one should be careful. It's nearly midnight on a dark deserted road."

"Well, the next road we come to, I'll turn off." He peered anxiously along the lighted way. "There seems to be some sort of an exit or driveway ahead. Maybe a road."

When they came to it, he said, "I'm going to turn in here and park at the end. We can get a little sleep, and I'll try to fix the problem as soon as it's light. Then we can be on our way." He turned into a narrow opening between two fences.

"It's against the law, isn't it? To camp like this?" asked Emily's mother.

"You're no help. What else can we do? It's an emergency." He was driving very, very slowly now, for the old road was rough.

"He has stopped!" said Emily. "The bearded man has stopped! I think he is going to follow us in."

"All right," said her father. "Now we can find out what he wants."

"No, he is turning around. He's going away," announced Emily.

"Thank heaven!" her mother said. "Now we have seen the last of him!"

It was clear the narrow old road was not used. The motor home — Emily's mother had named it the *Venturer* — jerked along over the old ruts. The headlights shone on tall grass and sprawling weeds growing in the middle of the road and along the edges. There were no houses in sight now, just fields on both sides. Along each side was a split-rail fence. Fifty feet farther there were trees that seemed to close the way.

"There's a sign," exclaimed Emily's mother. "Probably says 'No Trespassing'!"

Her father slowed so that the headlights fell on the sign.

"Can you make it out?" he asked.

Emily's mother spelled out the word on the sign. "I-n-n-i-s-f-r-e-e."

"What does it mean?" asked Emily.

"It's a garden, I think, in some faraway place," said her father.

"It's something in a book," her mother said. "There's a name underneath. Harrison, isn't it?" she asked her husband.

"That's what it looks like from here," he said. "Anyway, it says 'Owner .' "

"Let's get out of here," said Emily's mother.

"I can't risk it. What if I stall in the middle of some highway? There may be a house behind those trees at the end. We'll explain. I hope I can manage to get that far."

"Poor Edward," said Emily's mother. "You must be very tired. As soon as we stop, I'll make us all some hot drinks."

"There's another sign," said Emily. "It says, 'Dead End.'"

"We'll have to spend the night, so I will just park a little farther on, where we can't be seen from the road. We'll leave as soon as I find out what the trouble is."

When they had gone about fifty feet, they came to an open space, surrounded by trees glimpsed in the headlights.

The motor seemed to groan as Emily's father turned into the space. The trailer lurched slightly and stopped. "Wherever we are, this is where we spend the night." Emily's father turned the key and the groaning motor was silent. "I can't figure it out. Something is wrong with the engine. I paid that man near Ocala sixty-two dollars, and it still doesn't work right. I think it may be . . . perhaps it's . . . although . . . heaven forbid . . . I don't like it, I don't like it! It may be the alternator."

Emily peered out the window to see just where they were. Her mother switched on the inside lights.

"We'll go right to bed," said her father. "I must be up at dawn to get things moving. There's nothing I can do tonight."

He climbed outside with a flashlight to have a look. Emily slipped out behind him and ran out as far as the ring of light from the flashlight reached.

They were in a cleared place at the edge of a wood. There was no house, only a large tree not far away, and a flowering bush. She could hear water flowing, and there was also the sound of water rippling that came from the opposite direction and might be a brook.

"Come back, Emily," called her mother from the steps. "It's the middle of the night."

"I'm looking around."

"You can look tomorrow before we go."

"Something smells wonderful." Emily took a deep breath. "It's nice here. Why do we have to go tomorrow? Could we stay a little while, maybe for a few days?"

"We'll stay long enough to see what is the matter with the engine, anyway," her mother said. "It's time for bed."

"Can't I look at the stars for a minute?" Emily asked.

"For a minute. I'll make you a cup of cocoa." Her mother went inside.

Emily ran back along the overgrown road until there were no branches between her and the sky. She stood and stared at the small golden lights so far away. The sky was velvet. Her father came and stood beside her. He was sipping a mug of coffee.

"No matter what we lack," he said, "we have the stars."

"It's so big. It's so big," murmured Emily. "I'm going to study more about the stars."

"That's a good idea," said her father.

2
Early Next Morning

When Emily woke up she rolled over, and kneeling on her bunk, looked out of the little window beside her. She saw green trees whose quiet branches arched and met over a carpet of grass and clover and violets, and a river that wound away gently, widening in the distance as it flowed invitingly into a wood. She could scarcely believe her eyes, it was so beautiful.

"Where are we? Where is this?" she called in delight. "Mother, are you there?"

There was no answer from the other side of the curtain. She pulled on her blue robe. "Father!" she called. There still was no answer. She slipped her feet into straw slippers. They had bought them in New Mexico from the Indians last year. The slippers had no backs, so she had not outgrown them, but her heels hung over an inch.

Emily remembered that once, when the slippers were new, she had asked her father when they were going to settle down, and he had answered, "When we get to the promised land."

"Where is it?" she had asked.

"That I can't tell you," was his answer, "but we'll know it when we see it."

Now, as Emily padded to the door looking for her parents, something in her said, "This is the place."

Her father was outside drinking his coffee. Her mother was standing looking at the shining river that curved away into the greenness, murmuring over white coral stones as it ran. Beyond was a grassy bank, and not far away was a hedge of hibiscus.

"Father!" she called. "Father, I think it's our promised land! What do you think?" She rushed over to him.

He put his hand affectionately on her shoulder. "It certainly is something special," he answered.

Emily ran to her mother. "Mother, admit it's lovely," she said.

Emily's mother was looking across the grass at a magnificent magnolia tree some distance away, with cream-colored blossoms against shining dark green leaves. There was an old-fashioned wrought-iron bench beneath it. "Yes, it is a lovely place," she said after a minute.

Looking over her mother's head, Emily saw a flash of water in a lot across the road. "What is *that*?" she cried.

"It's an artesian well," her father said. "It gushes up from hundreds of feet underground and pours out like a fountain."

"Oh, I never saw anything more wonderful!" She rushed off to look at it more closely.

"Emily." Her mother's voice followed her. "Go in and wash and put on some clothes, then come out and have your breakfast."

Emily turned back. Her father was trying to start the engine, but the sounds were not encouraging.

Emily paused. "Wouldn't you like to stay here awhile, Mother?" she asked eagerly.

"I think I would. I like it as well as any place I've ever seen."

"Do you mean it? Father," she called, "did you hear that?"

"Yes, I did," he answered. "Did you mean it, Elvira?"

"What? That I like it here? Of course. It's really delightful. Pity we must leave before sundown."

"Oh, Mother, let's stay here always!"

"Darling, you know we can't. Why do you upset yourself? This land belongs to somebody else."

"How do we know it's not for sale?"

"We do know. Even if they would sell it, it would probably be more than we could afford."

"Emily, haven't you enjoyed the places we've been to?" her father asked. "Don't you like the *Venturer*?"

"Oh, I love it!" Emily said. "I know how lucky I am to have seen so many places. It's just that I wish we could go on vacation time, and have land of our own to come back to, like ordinary people."

Her father stroked her cheek. "I see what you mean." Then he said that the trouble with the engine was serious and went off to find a mechanic.

Emily and her mother set out to find the owner of the land to explain why they were there. They walked along the driveway to the road. Emily paused to get a closer view of the well as it poured into a wooden trough and found its way into the river about ten feet away. Sword bright, it flashed in the morning sun.

"I never imagined such a thing," she said.

"This does seem like a magical corner of the earth," her mother said.

"Magic! That's why we had trouble at this very place!" Emily said. "We were *supposed* to find it."

Emily's mother put her arm around Emily and patted the thin shoulder. "It is unusual," she said. "Your father is such a good driver, it's seldom that he gets lost."

"You're a good driver, too," said Emily.

"I can't compare with your father. Look for a mailbox, Emily. The house may be hidden in trees."

"I don't believe I could ever drive a car," said Emily.

"Oh, don't say that!" her mother exclaimed. "Everyone should learn to drive. It gives you wings. No one can manage properly without knowing how to drive. How would you get to the station or the bus, carry your suitcases, bring food from the market, take your children to school, pick up friends who come to see you? Think a minute."

"I won't go anywhere," Emily said. "I've ridden so much and so far, I'll just sit still for years."

Her mother laughed. "Well, thank your stars you've traveled. You'll have something to think about while you're sitting."

"Here's a mailbox," said Emily. "I guess that's the house." It was a white house with verandas, set in a splendid garden full of flowers. It seemed to be closed up, but a man was clipping a hedge. He looked up as they came, and waited for them to speak.

"Are you the owner?" Emily's mother asked.

"No, ma'am. Mr. Simeon Harrison is the owner."

"Could you tell us when he will be home?"

"He may be home any day now. He's been gone six months. He might be back any minute — or he might be away another six months."

"We broke down last night, and our motor home is parked off the road down there." Emily's mother made a gesture in the direction of the river.

The man looked at them without saying anything for a moment. He had a thin, peaked face, the skin stretched over the cheekbones. His eyes were hazel and sharp. He was dressed in blue jeans and a plaid cotton shirt. He said, "I guess it's all right if you broke down, but he wouldn't like anybody camping on his property."

"If he should come in, please tell him why we're there," said Emily's mother. "You don't know where we could reach him?"

"He may be in the jungles of the Amazon or the mountains of Borneo. I'm never sure." He went back to clipping off the hedge.

"What would he go to those places for?" Emily asked.

The man looked at her while he searched for an answer. "What does he go for? To find out things!"

"When he's found things out, what does he do then?" Emily persisted.

"Come along, dear," murmured her mother.

"He puts them in a book or a movie. Or he makes a speech about them."

"Where does he speak?" asked Emily.

"Wherever there's anybody who wants to hear about the things he's found out."

"Now, Emily," her mother said, "that's enough."

"My, she certainly can ask a lot of questions," said the man.

Emily looked back over her shoulder as her

mother drew her away. "Does his business take him to those places? What would you call a man like that?"

"An explorer," the man answered. "He's an explorer. That's his business. That's what he calls himself."

Emily waved her hand to thank him, and turned excitedly to her mother.

"Oh, Mother," she said. "since he's an explorer, and he's away so much, maybe he would sell us that little piece of land."

"Emily." Her mother laughed. "How would you find him to ask? The man said he could be anywhere. An explorer has the most unpredictable address in the world."

Emily walked along with her mother in silence, but her mind was full of questions.

3
The Secret Place

"Perhaps I could catch a fish for lunch," said Emily's mother when they reached the *Venturer.* "You had better study your lessons."

Emily's mother took a fishing pole from a closet and set it up near the shore. "Look at it every once in a while, Emily, and see if I have a strike. I have things to do inside."

Emily got her spelling book and went to sit on the weedy bank. It was very comfortable there on the grass, her back propped against the root of an oak tree.

Some small yellow flowers grew beside the river, and a clump of beautiful purplish blue flowers floated on the water. The river was deep, but rather narrow, and Emily could see a fish pass by now and then through the clear brown water. Across the water, the moss-hung woods were calm and inviting, and behind her the glade was lightened by flowering bushes and a few bright wildflowers. Emily remembered that the white flowers were spirea and the orange ones lantana.

The grass in the clearing had once been a lawn, although it had not been cut for some time, and clover blossoms, oxalis, and even some tall buttercups grew here and there, giving the place a welcoming air. Emily's book was unopened beside her.

She really didn't feel like studying. Was it only the day before yesterday, in St. Augustine, that the report from the correspondence school had come? Her father and mother had arranged to pick up their mail in care of general delivery, and they all had sat down to read their letters in the park, which had been laid out many hundreds of years ago.

Emily's mother had given her the big envelope from the school. "It must be your monthly tests," she said, "and next month's lessons."

"An A!" exclaimed Emily, taking out the papers. "More A's. I have an A-plus on my composition."

"You deserved it," said her father.

"But they say, 'Penmanship is sometimes hasty.' A-minus in arithmetic. Oh, dear, B. B-minus in science. I thought it was my best paper."

"You'll do better next time," her mother said.

When they had read all the mail, Emily's mother put the papers into her woven sling bag and gathered up the letters. They walked along the seawall in the direction of "the oldest house in America," according to the sign on the door.

Emily sat on a stool in the huge fireplace and made a wish. There was a saying that wishes made there often came true. Her father laughed. He said that wishes had a way of coming true even without a special place to wish them in.

"It was a hard wish to make," said Emily, "because I wished it alone. I should have wished that you and Mother wished it, too."

Now, sitting in the sun, sitting in the middle of her wish, Emily could feel the excitement she had felt in seeing St. Augustine. Her memories of the old streets were like a dream. The three of them had walked in and out of houses and gardens furnished and planted just as they had been two or three hundred years ago, all restored with loving care. Emily felt as though she had stepped into history.

About four o'clock at the end of that day, they had been on the road again. Emily tried to remember the events of that night and the next day that had led to their turning into the overgrown road with its dead end.

Emily's mother was driving and took the main highway out of St. Augustine. They had not found a place to stop until very late. It was a grubby little trailer camp. There were problems with the water, and Emily had to wash, as she sometimes had to when they were short of water, in a small tub. With a kettle of hot water to take the chill off, Emily washed herself bit by bit and dried off. Last, she put the tub on the floor for her feet and sat on the edge of her bunk. She felt very clean. It was good to lie in her bed all clean and in clean pajamas. She fell asleep happily.

They had made an early start. Her father always took the back roads, and as they went Emily saw that the woods alongside had changed into great live oaks hung with moss, a few pines, some holly, and low palmettos. These woods were open and inviting, not like the forbidding mangrove swamps, or the white cypresses with swollen roots that stood like threatening giants in tangled jungles that they passed in the northern part of the state.

At the gas station they were able to fill their water tanks, too. They passed through a little town that seemed built under the oak trees. There was even an ancient oak in the middle of the street, which divided around it. They saw a sign with an arrow pointing, "To the Beach."

"Oh, let's stop!" Emily said. "Follow that sign."

Emily's father turned into the road, which grew sandy as they went. Suddenly, there at the end, was the still, blue ocean stretching to the horizon. A half mile more and they reached the wide white sand and saw the waves breaking and foaming.

They parked on the side of the road in the sand dunes and walked to the beach. Emily's mother and father had put on their bathing suits, and Emily had squeezed into one that in six months had grown too small. She went barefoot, as she often did, but the sandspurs bothered her. Her father said she had better wear her sneakers after this, but Emily said she couldn't because she had lost one.

"Why didn't you tell us?" asked her mother. "I want to get you a new bathing suit, too." She sighed. "You're growing out of everything."

Emily ran over the sand and waded along the

edge of the ocean, letting the thin waves curl over her feet. She searched for shells and hoped that she might find some treasure that had been lost in a shipwreck and tossed up on the sand.

While she was gathering shells, the sky grew dark suddenly, and the waves became higher.

"We'll just rinse off," her mother said. "There's bad weather coming." She took Emily's hand and they ran into the water. "We must not go in too far. Feel the undertow," she said, and indeed, the sand was pulled from right under their feet. Emily rolled over and splashed about. Her mother took her hand, and they got out, pushing against the buffeting surf.

Before they reached the *Venturer*, the rain hit them. "I left my towel," Emily's father said.

"So did I," said Emily.

They rushed inside and closed the door.

The wind blew and the rain splashed against the windows as though they had been plunged under the sea. Emily had been in rainstorms before — in the New England Berkshires, in Texas, and in other places, but it seemed to her this storm was the worst. The lightning was so sharp and close, the thunder so loud, and the roar of the waves so ominous.

After the storm was over, they got ready to go on their way.

"Where are we going now?" asked Emily.

Her father handed some maps to her mother. "You can make up your mind as we ride along, dear," he said.

They had ridden through miles of orange groves, taken one back road after another, enjoying the country and the magnificent sunset. They had stopped to have something to eat and were off on back roads again. They passed through one or two little towns, but there seemed to be no place to stay for the night.

"Tomorrow we'll study the maps and get organized," Emily's father had said.

There had been trouble with the engine. They had come to the village with its charming row of shops in the tree-lined street. They had driven down the narrow road and turned in here. . . . Yes, that was how it was. Emily looked about happily.

It was as if she had come to a secret garden full of flowers, where birds sang and fountains splashed. At her feet was a very large flat rock. It was embedded in the bank, but the edge hung over the river. Emily slid down, inching her way along, to look into the clear, brown water. "This will be my rock!" she said to herself and curled up contentedly.

Her mother came back. "Child, dear, you are dreaming. Don't you see we've caught something?"

Emily's mother reeled in the line. It was a good-sized fish, but it flopped and fought and finally got away.

"Oh, dear," she exclaimed, "scrambled eggs! I was hoping to surprise your father, but it may surprise him anyway. He surely won't expect eggs for lunch again!"

She looked at Emily thoughtfully. "There's something you could do for me, dear, if you would. Could you walk up the road to those shops we saw? They can't be very far. I'd like cheese and fresh rolls, if they have them, and one or two other things."

"I'd love to!" Emily exclaimed. She took her book inside, and her mother put some money and the list of things to get in a little red purse. She gave the purse to Emily, cautioning her to walk well to the side of the road, and always on the side of the oncoming cars. "I always do," said Emily, impatiently.

It was not far. There were houses along the way — ten or twelve, counting both sides of the road, all with flowers or trees in the yards. Two or three larger houses were set back in carefully laid out gardens.

The shops, when she reached them, were almost all in one long block, under the arcade. Across the street, next to the small brick church, its door open invitingly, was a building that looked like a school.

A delicious smell of freshly baked bread was in the air, and Emily walked toward the bakery.

There was one other customer in the shop — a man. His back was toward Emily as she came in. As she came up to the counter, the man turned around, and she came face to face with him. She gasped. It was the man who had followed them last night in the car — the man with the beard!

Emily wanted to turn around and run, but she couldn't move.

"Good morning," the man with the beard said to her. "I don't think I've seen you around before." He smiled, and his voice was pleasant. Emily knew that her mother and father would want her to answer him. Why was she afraid? Yet it was near panic that made her turn and run out of the shop without saying a word.

Emily ran down the street and went into the open door of a shop that had piles of baskets at the entrance. She stood there breathing hard.

Why was that man still here, she asked herself, in this town? What had he wanted with them last night? Her father had said, "He is probably on his way somewhere, and is lost, the same as we are." But here he was buying bread like any ordinary person, so he hadn't been on his way anywhere.

Emily took a deep breath. Stop it, you are making it up, she told herself, as she often did when she began to get upset about things that had no answers. She stepped onto the street and headed back toward the bakery.

The bearded man was buying oranges at the fruit stand. He looked surprised to see Emily again and turned as though he would like to speak to her. But Emily pretended not to see him and went into the bakery. She bought a dozen fresh hot rolls and six cinnamon buns because they had just come in. She used her own money for the buns. It would be her present.

4
New Friends and New Shoes

Outside the bakery, Emily met a little boy. He looked at her with curiosity, then stepped in front of her, as though he would not let her pass. He had brown curly hair, and he was wearing red pants.

"Who are you?" he asked.

"I'm Emily Crump," she answered promptly, and waited for him to introduce himself. But the boy didn't.

"Where do you come from? What are you doing here?"

"I came in a motor home," Emily explained. "We are just down the road. And now I'm going to the grocery store." She tried to pass.

The boy looked at Emily for a moment, then stepped aside. Emily went on down the street and when she looked back, she saw the boy walking behind her. She was glad he seemed interested in her. Emily did her shopping quickly and hurried out of the store to see if he was waiting. He was, and with him was a girl about her own age.

"Who's that?" the girl asked, looking at Emily. She was pretty and plump, with dark curls and pink cheeks.

"She came in a trailer," the boy told her, "and she's buying groceries."

"We needed cheese and some other things," Emily volunteered, "and it's not a trailer, it's a motor home."

The girl stared. "What's her name?" she asked, as though Emily were some kind of animal in a zoo and couldn't speak for herself.

"Emily Crump," Emily answered quickly.

"Mine's Grace Pertible. My brother's name is Jason."

"Oh," said Emily. She couldn't think of anything else to say and started on down the street.

Grace and Jason walked along with her, one on each side. They never stopped talking. They lived not far away, they said, and wanted Emily to come and see their house. She thought she had better go straight home, as her mother was waiting for the groceries, but she thanked them for the invitation.

Grace said that she played the violin and that Jason played the violin and the piano besides. She said their father, when he was young, used to play in an orchestra, but now he had a law office. They had music every day at their house, and Emily could come if she wanted to.

Emily said she had often thought that it would be a fine thing to play the piano, but of course a violin would be easier to take about in a moving home. "But I've never held a violin in my hands," she said.

"I'll show you mine," said Grace. "How old are you?"

"I'm going on ten," answered Emily, wondering what that had to do with it, but Grace was thinking of something else.

"I guess we'll be in the same grade at school," she said. "I'll see you Monday."

"Where?" asked Emily. "Where will you see me? What is Monday?"

"School. Spring term. School begins Monday. See you!" They ran off.

Emily skipped and ran most of the way back

to the motor home. Her mother was busy in the little kitchen. Emily put the milk into the refrigerator and the bread into the painted breadbox.

"I'm invited to school," she announced. "It begins on Monday."

"Don't talk foolishly, dear. I'm in no mood."

Her father came in. "Well, Edward, what did they say? Where is the mechanic?"

"He'll be along, but he was doubtful when I told him it might be the alternator. He thinks he may have to send it to the city to have it fixed."

"But then when could they get it back?" Emily's mother asked. "We must be on our way. It makes me nervous to trespass."

"Just let's wait until he has seen it, but I imagine it may take about a week."

Emily began to dance. "Then can't I go to school while we wait? Can't I? Can't I?"

"You can't go to school for only a week," her mother said. "School is a serious business. You must enroll for a whole year."

"Then let's stay here, and I'll go for a year. It's the prettiest town!"

"Even now, we may be in trouble for trespassing," said her father mildly.

"Oh, please, just think about it! The Green Circle is so beautiful!"

"What green circle?" her mother asked.

"*Our* Green Circle! Here, where we are. Look out the door. See how the land curves, and the water goes around it."

"We can't stay on land belonging to someone else," her mother said. "We'd all be put in the hoosegow."

"Then let's buy it!" Emily said.

"Oh, *Emily*," said her mother.

Emily's hopes faded. "Well," she said in a sad little voice, "I'd better go outside and enjoy it while I have it."

"Please, darling, stay within call," her mother said. "You may not go into the woods unless you are shod."

"Unless I'm what?"

"Shod. Unless you have your shoes on."

"Oh, like a horse! I've heard that word. Then may I put on my good shoes?"

"No, but I'll buy you some new sneakers today," her mother said. "As soon as I've finished here, we'll go and find a shop. I may not have enough money. Give me about twenty dollars, please, Edward."

Emily's father frowned slightly, but put his hand into his pocket. "What's the matter with those rubber things from Japan, with the thong between the toes that we bought for her?"

"She can't wear them in the woods," Emily's mother said. "They are fine around the house. But she needs a new pair of those, too. And I'll see if they have any bathing suits."

He handed her the money, which she put into her purse. "Thank you, dear," she said. "Oh — I forgot about the garage bill. Can we manage?"

He nodded. "That won't break us."

Emily's mother looked at Emily. "Comb your hair, dear, before we go out. It's as wild as a wintry sea."

Emily went to the mirror that hung in a little space near the dining table. She took a comb and brush from a wooden box that had once held some gadget of her father's and smoothed her hair. Then she went outside to wait for her mother.

She began to gather up the fallen sticks and leaves that cluttered up the special place by the river that she already called her own. She had put them all in a neat pile by the time her mother was ready to go.

Emily had to put on her socks and her good shoes and to wash her feet first. Then they started off.

Emily carried a shopping basket for her mother. It was a pretty basket with a pattern of running horses, made by the Indians. Everything Mother has is pretty, Emily thought proudly.

There seemed to be no shoe shop in the village, but a sort of general store had a shoe section. "Have you sneakers or some sort of sandal that would fit this child?" Emily's mother asked.

"No, ma'am, we sure haven't," was the reply. They didn't have bathing suits, either. After visiting one or two places, they found sneakers in the grocery store. Emily tried them on and her mother paid for them. Once they were outside, she decided that Emily had better wear the sneakers home to save her best shoes from the white dust of the road.

"I don't have to wear *any* shoes just to walk in a road," said Emily, but her mother didn't answer, so Emily sat on a packing box near the grocer's and changed her shoes. She wrapped the ones she had been wearing and put them in the bottom of the basket.

"I didn't wear any shoes this morning," she said.

"I'm sorry about that," said her mother. "Now what shall we take to your father?" It was a custom of the Crumps that whenever one of them went out, he or she brought something for the ones left behind.

On this trip, Emily's mother bought tangerines, and Emily spent her own money for a black ink pen in a cellophane wrapper.

Emily's mother stopped at a small display of seed packages. "I think I'll buy a package of these morning-glory seeds, and the nasturtiums, too. I'll plant them just for fun. It will be a gift to the owner. He will be surprised by blue morning glories one fine day. It's always nice to leave a place better than you found it."

On a stand were seedlings in packs. The little plants already had flowers on them. "I can't resist these impatiens," said Emily's mother. "No trouble to stick them in the ground. That's such a lovely color." She paid for them.

"Carry the plants for me, Emily, and I'll take the basket," she said.

Emily's father was cleaning out the runnel at the artesian well when Emily and her mother returned. The runnel originally had flowed right into the river, but it had become so clogged with leaves and weeds that the water spilled out over the ground, making a marsh of that part of the meadow. Edward had succeeded in making a V-shaped channel of stones to coax the water back. He gave them a triumphant smile.

"Looks better, doesn't it?" he asked proudly.

His face was red from effort, his hair rumpled, his shoes muddy. "The man came from the garage," he told them. "He will do his best to hurry the job, but it may be a few days. We will need this water."

"Look at these colors." Emily's mother showed him the load of vegetables — purple eggplant, a spray of carrots, blossoms of artichokes and lettuce, and crookneck squash arching swanlike from the basket. "There are times when I wish I could paint."

"It would be better if *I* could paint," said Emily's father. "Then I could put you in the picture."

Emily's mother smiled.

"Is it all right for me to go out for a while?" said Emily. "I just want to see something over there."

"All right," said her father.

"I'll be safe," said Emily, laughing. "I'm shod."

5
Emily Talks with a Fascinating Stranger

Emily followed an overgrown path away from the stream, through a little grove of trees toward the road. The Harrison house should be in that direction. She decided that she would just look about to see if there was any sign of the explorer.

A few pines grew among the oak and sweet gum trees, and there were clumps of azaleas making pools of color under the trees. Gray moss dripped from the branches, mournful and mysterious. Palmetto bushes grew here and there. The narrow path at times was almost lost in the underbrush, but finally led up to an opening in the hedge behind the shuttered house that she had visited earlier with her mother.

The man they had spoken with was nowhere to be seen, but there were noises coming from a little shed not far away.

Emily slipped along the hedge and saw the man through the glass wall of the shed. He was putting a group of strange plants into larger pots. He knocked them out of the smaller pots by hitting the clay edges to loosen the earth. That was the sound she had heard.

She stood enjoying the garden and wondering whether she would speak to the gardener. There were many fascinating plants all around. Beside her was a clump of white flowers of a kind she had never seen before. She looked at them so that she could describe them to her father, and in them she imagined that she saw the face of a little lion. It was a white face, since it was made of flowers, but the eyes were dark and sad, made of shadows. The mouth was a dark smile. How did the light and shadow gather together to make such a dear little face? She wished that the lion would spring out of the flowers and play with her, but just then a breeze ruffled the petals and the lion's face disappeared.

Then she saw that there was somebody else in the garden. Not far from her, a tall young man was staking up a huge camellia bush. He had on gray slacks, and a white shirt with the sleeves rolled up. He wore canvas shoes, the kind used on boats. He did not notice her.

"Are you a gardener?" Emily asked finally.

He turned, startled, his blue eyes open wide.

"Where did you come from?" he asked.

She waved her hand. "Over there. Are you a gardener?"

"I'm not much of a gardener, I'm afraid, but I love a garden."

"I do, too," said Emily, "and I like to know the name of everything in it."

He looked at her, interested. "Yes, so do I. *You* are in a garden. What's *your* name?"

"Emily. Emily Crump."

"You're new here, aren't you?"

She nodded. "We've just come."

The man sat down on a garden bench. "Whew, I'm done in! Sit down if you like." The man pulled a shiny leaf from a large bushy tree behind the bench and offered it to her. "Smell it — crush it. It's a camphor tree. People use camphor for healing."

Emily took the leaf and sat down on the end of the bench. She crushed the leaf and smelled it. It was sharp and pleasant. There was a faint feeling of oil on her fingers. "I like it," she said. "Tell me the name of something else. Are you new in this town, too?"

"Oh, no. We were early settlers," the man said. "And let me see. The name of something. Those are oleanders." He waved his hand toward a row of tall flowering bushes, pouring pink color from their moving tops. "They are poison. Best stay away from them. There are many, many plants in Florida that one should only look at, and many berries that should be passed by. Lovely to look at, and quite harmless if you only look."

"Poison ivy is the one I know," said Emily. "I was born in New England, and we have a lot of it there."

"We have some of it here, too. But it's all been rooted up out of these woods."

"Because people wanted to leave the woods better than they found them, I suppose."

He looked at her, startled, and then smiled. "Well, as I said, my family has been in Florida a long time. I had a great-uncle who was a barefoot postman."

"Do you mean it — what you just said?" asked Emily, wondering if he was teasing her.

"I do. Yes, he usually carried his shoes hung around his neck. He went between Palm Beach and Miami, and it took three days walking along the ocean to go sixty-six miles. Of course, it was easier to walk barefoot. He walked on the hard sand along the beaches, because roads had not yet been built, and there was no other way to get there."

Emily pictured the wide, lonely beaches stretching into the distance.

"He took something to cook in," the man went on, "and a few supplies in a knapsack. He'd find turtle eggs or oysters, drink coconut milk, eat the heart of a palm, or catch a fish for supper. Have you ever eaten turtle eggs or hearts of palm?"

"Not yet," answered Emily. "But I've walked on the beaches barefoot. I love having the waves wash over my feet when I look for shells. Where did the barefoot postman sleep?"

"Usually in the sand high up on the beach, where it is soft; sometimes sheltered by coconut palm branches or a tree limb that hung low."

"He was brave," she said. "Wasn't he lonely?"

"Yes, he must have been, sometimes. But once in a while he would let a traveler walk along with him. Someone who just *had* to go to Miami, or perhaps someone on the way north.

"Once in a while, even, he might take two or three. He would be paid something for guiding them and helping them to catch their food. But I guess they were a great trouble to him, for he was used to striding along on a certain rhythm, to arrive on time, and I suppose it wasn't always easy to persuade people to keep up with him."

"It explains why some people like to take their houses with them, doesn't it?"

"It's not the same thing at all. By his courage, by accepting difficulties, by facing life alone and unaided, my great-uncle helped open up lower Florida, and so he made life there possible for those who came after him."

The other man came out of the shed just then. He spoke as he came toward them. "Mr. Harrison, do you want to look at these plants? I've just finished repotting them."

"Yes, I do, Bruce. Thank you."

Emily looked at the man in astonishment. "Are you Mr. Harrison?"

"Yes, I'm Simeon Harrison; who did you think I was?"

"But he said you were away exploring."

"I came back an hour ago. I've enjoyed our little talk. I'll see you again sometime. Good-bye." But she continued to stare at him, and it puzzled him. "Good-bye," he said again.

Emily just stood there for a moment. She

knew that she might not see Mr. Harrison again, and there was a question she was burning to ask. "I'd like to know something about exploring," she said.

"What would you like to know?"

"How do you do it?"

Mr. Harrison considered her question.

"Well," he said, "you go places — mostly hard-to-get-to places. Say there's a place you've wondered about, and you try to find out all about it, but nothing you read tells you what you want to know, so you just have to go there. So while you're there you find out its history, what used to be there, what's there now — sometimes you have to dig it up out of the earth. It might be where an ancient city once was. You make notes about everything you find out, so that you get it exactly right, and you take pictures so that you can share your adventure with other people."

"This last place you've just come back from — where was that?"

"I was in the Arctic, photographing under the ice."

"You're teasing me," said Emily.

Mr. Harrison laughed. "No, that's where I was. It was very strange and wonderful. They cut a big hole through the ice, and I went down. It's very cold, so you can't stay long."

The man called Bruce interrupted. "Mr. Harrison, if you don't mind, would you look at these plants so I can go to lunch?"

"I'm sorry, Bruce, I didn't mean to hold you up." He looked at Emily. "I'll tell you another time . . . er . . . what is your name again?"

"Emily Crump." She walked along with him toward the shed. "What's it like down there, under the ice?"

"It's more beautiful and strange than any experience I've ever had. It's the most exciting spot on earth. You'd stay forever, only after a while you couldn't breathe."

Bruce now claimed his attention. "Mr. Harrison, I'd like to order a few dozen peat planters and some stakes and a few other things. I've made a list."

Mr. Harrison nodded and they went into the shed.

"Good-bye," she called, looking after them.

"Another time," said Mr. Harrison carelessly over his shoulder.

Emily ran all the way home.

* * * *

"Mr. Harrison has come back," Emily announced, flinging herself through the door.

Her mother was making a cake.

"What does he look like?" she asked.

"Very nice. Smart. I talked to him."

"Emily, you didn't say anything about us? About our being on his land, did you?"

"No."

"That was good. You'd better let your father handle it."

Emily turned to her father. "He's really nice," she said. "I'm sure if you told him how much we love the Green Circle, there would be some way to buy it. Couldn't we try?"

Her father and mother looked at each other.

"It *is* a lovely spot, and one place is not much more different from another," said Emily's mother at last.

Her husband looked at her in astonishment. "Are you saying that you would be willing to settle down in this village? Take a chance on getting to know people?"

"I'm not sure how I feel about that," Emily's mother answered truthfully. "I don't think we have much chance of getting it anyway."

There was a delicious smell of vanilla from the cake batter. Emily perched on a stool and watched.

"It seems like a good time for a little celebration," her mother said.

"Will it have icing?" Emily asked hopefully.

"Certainly. Go find the birthday candles, dear."

"Whose birthday is it?" Emily asked, her mind whirling around possible answers.

"Why, your Great-Great-Great-Grandmother Wigglesworth. She would be two hundred and thirty-two years old today. I think I'll use pink and white icing."

"If we are going to have a party, could I ask somebody to come?" She brought the box of small candles to the table.

"Do you know anyone?" her father asked, surprised.

"Two children who spoke to me when I went to get the groceries."

"Then I'll get out Grandmother Wigglesworth's blue and white Canton plates," said her mother. She poured the batter into a pan she had prepared with buttered wax paper and put it carefully into the oven.

Emily jumped up. "I'll go and see if I can find Grace and Jason."

"Wouldn't you like to put on a dress for the party?" her mother suggested. Emily thought about it. She didn't often wear a dress.

"I might," Emily said. She owned two dresses. She took one from the closet she called hers — a small section of the row of closets across the back of the motor home. There weren't many clothes. Blue jeans and shorts were all they seemed to need.

Emily went into the shower room. It was fitted something like an airplane, a compact toilet and wash basin and a shower. She hung the dress on a hook. It was a pale green dress with flowers and a lace collar. She washed her face and hands, and combed her hair.

"I'm going as I am," said Emily. "I'll put on the dress when I come back. Please, could we have the awning up?" The awning of red and white stripes could be fastened on the outside of the motor home to make a porch, and it could be closed with a front flap to make a dressing room for swimmers when they were near the ocean. Emily was moving so fast that she was already outside and had to stick her head inside the door again to hear the answer.

"Why not?" replied her father.

6
Emily Meets the Pertibles

Emily couldn't find the Pertibles at first. She was about to give up when she saw Jason trying to fly a kite in an empty lot. He wasn't having much success as there was very little wind. He saw her and began to roll up the string. She explained that she wanted him and his sister to come to a party later that afternoon.

"Where do you live?" he asked.

Emily thought. Where *did* she live? She asked him if he knew where Mr. Harrison's house was. "Well, just before you come to it, there's an old road. We're in back."

"Maybe we'll come," he said, "but you'll have to come with me to my house and ask my mama."

Emily thought that it would be fun to see where Jason and Grace lived, so she went with him. They came to a brick house with a brick path leading to the front door, and set in a carelessly tended garden crowded with shrubs and flowers. Jason opened the low white gate and ran up the walk between strips of petunias and ageratum. He flung open the front door. "Come on," he said.

There was a large bowl of flowers under a mirror on a table at one side, and Emily saw that there were glass doors at the other end of the hall, which opened onto a bright space full of flowers and green. Jason pushed her into a room at the right, where a big handsome woman was sitting beside an open window sewing on something pink.

"Mama," said Jason in a breathless way, "here's that girl I told you about."

The woman rose. "What's her name?" she asked in just the way Grace had asked.

Jason couldn't remember. He looked at Emily, and Emily, for a moment, couldn't remember, either. Mrs. Pertible and Jason looked at her expectantly.

"Oh. It's Emily," she said, "Emily Crump."

"How do you do?" said Mrs. Pertible, offering her hand. "I hope you'll stay for lunch?"

"Well, I'd like to," said Emily doubtfully. "I just came to ask if Grace and Jason could come to a party this afternoon. My mother has made a cake."

"That sounds delightful," said Mrs. Pertible. "I'm sure they would love to come." As she walked back across the room her long skirt, made of yards and yards of cotton material, moved with a swaying motion. Emily wondered if Mrs. Pertible wore this dress on the street.

"Jason," said his mother, "go and tell your father that lunch will be ready in five minutes, and tell him that we have a visitor." She waved Emily to a chair opposite hers and resumed her sewing. As she worked, she smiled, but more to herself than to Emily.

Emily looked about her. The room had long windows that opened like doors onto a side veranda shadowed at one end by a wisteria vine. There was an enormous mirror in a gold frame that covered all one side of the room. Reflected in the mirror were a piano and metal stands for holding music. There were flowers in vases of several shapes and sizes and, near her, a lifelike marble bust of a man with a stern, sad face was set on a pedestal. She wondered who it was.

"Beethoven," said Mrs. Pertible, seeing her staring.

"Oh," said Emily. "He has something to do with music, hasn't he?"

"He has, indeed," cried Mrs. Pertible. "Would you care for a little music before luncheon?"

"I guess so," Emily answered.

At that moment Jason came in with his father. Mr. Pertible was a rather small, nervous man who wore glasses. Emily was introduced. "How do you do?" she said.

"How are you, young lady?" he said. "I hear you're a visitor in our town." He sat down near her and crossed his legs, swinging one foot back and forth in the air while he talked. "Where is Grace?" he asked. No one answered, but Jason left the room.

"So you live in a motor home," remarked Mr. Pertible. "They say Americans travel all the time and want to go everywhere sitting down, and so I suppose some people want to take their houses with them, too!"

Mrs. Pertible sat smiling, her skirt flowing around her. She reminded Emily of a pincushion.

"Where are you folks from?" Mr. Pertible asked.

She answered, "My father and I were born in New England, but my mother is from Canada. They had wheat as far as the eye could see on every side."

"Did you mention what your father does?" Mr. Pertible asked.

"Does? Did? Before he married my mother, do you mean? He had a little store. He sold screws and bolts and things like that."

"Sounds like a useful kind of store to keep."

"It was started by my grandfather, so after he died my father kept on with it. When I was about four years old, my mother wanted to travel, so he sold the store and bought a motor home."

"What does he do now?"

"He can do anything."

"Yes, but what does he *do*?"

Emily considered Mrs. Pertible's question. She was so curious herself, about everyone, and asked so many questions, that it seemed perfectly natural for everyone else to be interested in her family.

"You'd be surprised how much there is to do," she confided. "He always thought that he could write a book if he traveled, but he doesn't have much free time. He has some of it done, though."

"What kind of book?"

"He didn't tell me. He says now that writing is just like everything else, and you just have to settle down to it."

"I guess that's true of everything," said Mr. Pertible.

"Do you go to school?" asked Mrs. Pertible.

"Yes, I go to school in Baltimore."

"Boarding school?"

"No, by mail. I've already had two certificates," Emily added proudly. "I have lessons with my father and mother."

"Do you like that way of doing things?" Mr. Pertible asked.

Emily was thoughtful. "Well . . . I might like lessons in a real school a little better. I mean, a school with real people in it. As it is, I have to imagine them. I'd like to live in a village like this with friends I'd never have to change."

Grace came in with Jason. "Hi!" she said.

Mrs. Pertible rose. "Now we'll have some music," she said.

Jason and Grace went at once to a table near the piano, opened two long dark cases, and took out their violins. Emily jumped up, and Grace showed her the instrument, but did not let her touch it. It seemed a strange thing to Emily, and rather beautiful. Certainly, when she had heard music on television, the musicians had played on contraptions like these. She was sorry that she hadn't paid more attention.

Mr. Pertible also took a violin from a case. It was larger and had a longer neck. He stood a little apart, and set up a sheet of music on one of the metal stands. Grace and Jason waved their bows in the air.

"Mozart," said Mr. Pertible.

"Beethoven," corrected Mrs. Pertible, seating herself at the piano. "Emily wants to hear Beethoven. We'll do the Sonata, Opus Twelve in A major, the third movement — the finale."

Grace took the music from the pile on the piano, gave a sheet to her father and put one before Jason.

Their mother thumped a note on the piano. Grace and then Jason drew their bows across the strings. Then they wound up the strings on little knobs at the neck of the instrument. Grace played a few notes. Mr. Pertible didn't make any sound on his violin, and Emily saw that it had no strings.

Mrs. Pertible ran her fingers over the keys. She nodded her head. The children played. Emily

walked backward until she reached a chair and slipped into it. She was enthralled. It was not only the music that charmed her, but the sight of a family concentrated on a project together. She wished that there was something that she and her mother and father could do together.

She watched Mr. Pertible. He was playing more enthusiastically than any of them, but no sound came from his violin. His right hand, holding the bow in delicate fingers, made long sweeping movements through the air, and the supple fingers of his left hand were as quick as white mice. She tried not to stare at him as he played on no strings, nodding his head, moving his graceful arms, his lips pursed with the melody, but never adding a sound.

The music stopped.

"Beautiful, just beautiful," murmured Mrs. Pertible. "Jason, we'll play that passage that went wrong." She counted the bars on the music before her. "You went off —"

"I know. I know where it is," said Jason. He lifted his violin. Mrs. Pertible played the passage. His violin answered.

"Better," said Mrs. Pertible. She swung around. "Emily, I could see that you were puzzled by Mr. Pertible's violin. He wants to hear how the children play, and he can listen better when he is part of the performance. He is like the conductor of an orchestra. He sets the time and we follow him. The way he moves his hands says 'louder' or 'softer,' 'faster' or 'slower.' "

"Why, that's wonderful!" said Emily.

"It's his own idea," said Mrs. Pertible proudly. "Of course, if he added the *sound* of his violin, it would change the whole effect of the music."

"I see," said Emily. She felt as if she were being told important secrets and had been admitted to a world she had not known existed.

Mrs. Pertible smiled at her. "Let's have lunch now," she said. She sailed from the room.

The children and their father put away their instruments. Grace took Emily by the hand and all went into the dining room.

There were flowers on the table and straw mats at each place. There was milk in blue glasses before each child. There was a great bowl of vegetable salad in front of Mrs. Pertible. She served Emily, and Mr. Pertible added a lump of cottage cheese. Hot buttered rolls were in a silver dish covered with a napkin, and when they were passed to her, Emily didn't know whether she should uncover them or slip her hand under the napkin. "No, thank you," she said to be safe.

"Nonsense," said Mrs. Pertible. "They are good for you." She flung back a corner of the napkin, and Emily took a roll. Everything was delicious.

The Pertibles talked a lot while they were eating. They laughed, they shouted sometimes, they contradicted each other. Once in a while one of them spoke to Emily, but she was content to watch and to listen. There was no dessert. Mrs. Pertible and Jason began to clear the table, and Emily followed Grace into the living room. Mr. Pertible had disappeared. In a few minutes Mrs. Pertible came in and took up her sewing.

Emily was looking at a little bump that had appeared some time before on her index finger. "Come here, child," commanded Mrs. Pertible. She looked at the finger. "You have a little wart there," she said, indicating a tiny, three-sided lump. "Why don't you go in and ask Henry to rub it for you?"

Emily wondered if Henry could be Mr. Pertible. Mrs. Pertible seemed to read her mind. "Henry is the cobbler," she explained. "He has a repair shop on Main Street."

"It's not hard to find," Grace said. "Henry is on the same block as the bank. I'll show you."

"I must go home and tell my mother that you

and Jason are coming to the party." She turned to Mrs. Pertible. "Thank you very much for my lunch. I've had a lovely time. Oh, and the music! It was wonderful."

"You are very welcome, dear. Come again." She put her sewing down and opened the front door. There was a big bed of pansies blooming at the side of the house. "Help yourself to some pansies," suggested Mrs. Pertible, as she was closing the door. "The more you pick pansies, the better they like it, and the faster they bloom." She smiled, and the door closed.

How could that be? Emily wondered. It seemed against nature. But she gathered the pansies happily, and Grace picked some, too, which she added to Emily's bunch. Then they walked along together.

7
A Riddle

Emily felt that she was really becoming part of the village. She wondered about Henry and what a wart had to do with repairing shoes. There was a rule that she always consulted her parents before she went anywhere, but this was on the way home, so she thought she would just stop and see if she could get a clue to Mrs. Pertible's suggestion. She would have asked Grace, but she didn't know what to ask her.

They came to the corner. Just as they turned into the Main Street, an old-fashioned black convertible was passing. The driver had a beard — it was *that* man again.

"Grace, look quickly," Emily said. "Do you know that man? Have you seen him before?"

"Of course. He lives here. I guess everybody knows him."

"Are they scared of him?"

"Scared of him?" Grace asked. "Why would they be? But come to think of it, I guess some people may be. I hope he hasn't been to see your family?"

"No, no, I just wondered. What's his name? Tell me about him. What does he do?"

"I'll tell you about him," Grace said, "but you have to guess what he does. Here's the first clue: Most of the time, people are not glad to see him when he comes to their houses, yet often they call him up and ask him to come back."

Emily thought about that. "I can't imagine."

"Guess," Grace said, enjoying her game. "They may be sorry to see him come, but he sometimes leaves them happier."

"It sounds impossible. Tell me what he does. Why are they sorry to see him come?" Emily asked.

"He hurts them sometimes."

"So they don't like him?" Emily couldn't figure it out.

"I didn't say that," Grace said with a laugh. "They love him."

"Grace, you're making it up! Tell me something else about him."

"Well, he loves flowers, and when he has the time he weeds in his garden. He has someone to dig for him."

"Why?"

"He is careful of his hands. He lives alone. His wife died about a year ago. It made him very sad."

"I still can't guess," Emily said. "Tell me. Does he go to his business?"

"Half the time. Half the time his business comes to him."

They were in front of a low building. "The shoemaker is just up these stairs," said Grace. "Think about it. The answer is so easy!" She ran toward her home. "See you later!"

"Come about three o'clock," called Emily.

The entrance to the shop was through a narrow doorway and up a short flight of stairs. There was a sign in the hall — "Shoes Made or Mended" — and a small arrow pointed upward.

She entered the shop. It was a large bright room without any blinds or shutters. There were two straight chairs for customers, and behind a high counter — upon which a dozen or more pairs of shoes were neatly arranged — sat a black man bending over his work. At his side was an old cobbler's bench, some leather, and a number of tools. The man wore very heavy glasses, and as Emily came toward him, he took them off, as if to see her better.

"What can I do for you?" asked Henry. His voice was warm and the syllables were slurred in the way that most people in the town talked.

"I came to ask if you would rub my wart," Emily answered.

He put down his work and reached a hand to her. "Let me see that wart," he said.

Emily held out her finger across the bench.

He nodded, turning the finger over. Then he began to rub it lightly. "Uh-hum, uh-hum," he murmured. "You've had that wart a long time," he said as he continued to rub, "and you've thought about it a lot. Now I don't want you to think about it anymore. And one day, maybe tomorrow, maybe today, you'll look at a certain tree or you'll be crossing the street, and you'll say, 'Whatever happened to my wart?' and it'll be gone." He gave the wart another light rub, patted her hand lightly, and returned it to her.

"Thank you," she said.

"Don't think about it," said Henry.

"I won't," she promised. "Would you like to have some of my pansies?"

Henry picked up the shoe he had been working on. "If you'll pour a little water from that bottle into the tin cup there." She put the water and some of the pansies into the tin cup and set it on the counter where he could see it.

"My mother always kept a big bed of pansies," said the cobbler. "They take me back."

Emily went out quietly.

8
An Uninvited Guest

Emily saw that everything was ready for the party. The camping table and chairs were set up under the awning. There was a flower at every place.

"It looks so pretty!" she exclaimed. Her mother was setting little glass dishes for the ice cream on blue and white plates. "Grace and Jason are coming," Emily said, and began to tell her mother about everything that had happened at the Pertibles. "The music was wonderful! It was by Beethoven. Did you ever hear of him?"

"Oh, yes. You must remember to tell your father," Emily's mother replied. "The Pertibles certainly sound interesting."

"Oh, these are for you." Emily gave her mother the rest of the pansies she and Grace had picked. She noticed her mother had put on a dress, and Emily wanted to be just like her. "I'm going to wear my pink dress this afternoon," she said, "instead of the green one." She went to the closet and took it out.

Emily's mother put the pansies in water in a deep blue bowl as Emily went off to take a shower.

She peeled off her blue jeans and T-shirt and hung them in the closet. She showered quickly. Then she took down the green dress from the hook in the shower room and put it back on the hanger. She leaned against her mother, and her mother pulled up the zipper in the back of the pink dress.

Grace and Jason arrived just then. They had put on clean clothes, too.

Emily took them around the Green Circle and to her special place by the river. "This is my rock," she said. "I study my lessons here." She was pretending that she had lived there a long time. Jason promptly climbed the oak tree.

"I'll come by for you on Monday," said Grace. "We can go to school together."

"That'll be fine," said Emily.

"I'm glad you've come, Emily. I have been looking for a best friend."

"So have I," said Emily.

Jason dropped out of the tree. "Let's go inside," he said.

"Why?"

"I'd like to see what it looks like."

The Pertibles had never met anyone who lived in a motor home before, so Emily showed them all the workings of compact living: the neat row of closets, the kitchen, painted a powder blue, the dining area where her bed was. They were fascinated with the way the dining table folded away and there was her bunk. There was a daytime couch that turned into a double bed at night when the folding curtain was drawn to make it a bedroom. There was her mother's dressing table, which Emily's father had built in for her.

Emily explained that the lights could be hooked up to the electricity of a town through a camping site, or they could use their own power. They also carried — for emergencies — a kerosene lamp with a mantle that gave a good light.

The shower room was tiled. Grace thought it would be hard to dress in such a small space. Emily told her how her father often rigged up an outside shower, but here, of course, there was water from a flowing well. It was delicious to drink, too, she remarked, even if it did have an odd taste and was very cold. Grace admitted that the smell was strange and strong, but said Emily would get used to it. "This is like a wonderful doll's house!" said Grace.

Emily's mother put the cake on the table outside. Her father arrived and shook hands with Emily's guests. The guests were allowed to light the candles: a candle for each generation.

"Whose birthday is it?" asked Jason, looking around.

"It's my Great-Great-Great-Great-Grand-mother Wigglesworth's birthday," Emily's mother told them. "She would be two hundred and thirty-two years old today. I'm not sure exactly how many 'greats' there are!"

"Is she alive now?" asked Jason politely. He thought anything was possible with these unusual people.

"Oh, no, I'm sorry to say, but she did live to an old age. She was very beautiful and small. This china belonged to her. It was brought back from the Orient by her son, who was a sea captain." Emily's mother looked with pride at the blue and white dishes. She poured lemonade into the glasses, and Emily's father passed the finger-sized sandwiches. There were paper napkins and small dishes of nuts.

They played a game called "Hiding." Emily explained it. You thought of a place within sight, and you said whether you were large or small, and when you said, "I am hid," the others had to guess where. Grace hid in the top of a rose near the candle on the cake, and Jason in the oleander near the fence. Emily hid on a brown log in the stream.

Then Emily's mother brought out the ice cream, and they cut the cake. Everyone was given a large slice. It was a yellow-gold pound cake.

"It smells delicious," said Grace.

"It tastes delicious, too," said Emily. "It's my favorite. Nobody makes cakes like my mother."

"It's Grandmother Wigglesworth's own recipe," said Emily's mother. "She had wonderful recipes. I sometimes think of putting them into a book."

"This is the best pink ice cream I ever tasted," said Jason.

"Thank you," Emily's mother said. "I make it in the ice trays with real cream and fresh strawberries. Have some more. There's plenty." She gave him another huge spoonful.

Now they played a game Emily called "Remembering." What are the ten most beautiful things in the world? . . . Remember a time when you were very brave. . . . If you were marooned on a desert island, what three things would you like to take with you? . . . The Pertibles giggled and shouted and interrupted, behaving as they had in their own home. Emily could tell that they were having a good time. Then Emily's father sang some songs, and her mother, in a clear sweet voice, sang old English ballads. The three children and Emily's father joined in. Their voices rose in the air and floated over the treetops.

Simeon Harrison heard the laughter and the singing in the distance. "What's going on?" he asked the gardener, Bruce.

"I don't hear anything," said Bruce.

"Then listen."

"Oh! It must be those people in the camper," said Bruce.

"What people? Where?"

"They're parked down by the river."

"By the creek. On my land!" exclaimed Mr. Harrison. He was suddenly very angry. No one had any respect for private property anymore. They hadn't asked *him* if they could camp there.

In his anger he did not remember that he had been away. He strode through the woods behind his house toward the river. Bruce was sorry that he hadn't mentioned to Mr. Harrison that the strangers had had a breakdown, but he didn't like to speak to him when he was angry. He knew that his employer was always quick to get over his resentment.

Simeon Harrison was thinking that people had no right to be singing and laughing if they were trespassing. They were enjoying themselves at his expense. Well, he would soon put a stop to it.

As he came out of the woods, a merry sight was before him: the motor home, with its bright striped awning; a table decorated with pansies; a cake with lighted candles. Around the table sat five people eating ice cream and singing a song about "waters ripple and flow." It was so happy and unexpected that somehow Mr. Harrison felt angrier than ever. He approached the table.

Jason looked up and saw him. "Hello, Mr. Harrison!" he said.

"Do I know you?" asked Mr. Harrison, scowling. He was in such a bad mood that he didn't see any of the faces clearly.

"Yes, I'm Jason Pertible, and that's Grace."

"What are you doing here with these people?" Mr. Harrison asked gruffly.

"We were invited." Jason was worried. Something was wrong. He couldn't say what. He began to eat his ice cream faster.

"May we offer you some ice cream and cake, Mr. Henderson?" asked Emily's mother.

"It's Harrison!" he answered — and then added, "Thank you."

"Good-bye," said Jason, getting up from the table. "I had a very nice time."

"Take your cake, Jason, and eat it on the way home," Emily's father suggested. He wrapped the cake in a paper napkin, and Jason was off in an instant.

"I'll walk to the end of the road with them," said Emily.

Her mother nodded. "That's a good idea."

"We had a lovely time," said Grace quickly, and then she and Emily ran after Jason, leaving Emily's parents to face the angry Mr. Harrison.

9
Emily Hears Some Bad News

Emily went with the Pertibles until they were in sight of the shops. Jason soon finished his cake, and the three children raced along the road. Both the Pertibles could run faster than Emily. They turned and waved and went on toward home.

Emily was sorry she didn't have a chance to say good-bye, and she was embarrassed that the party had broken up like that. She stood looking after Grace and Jason, hoping that she would see them again. She didn't like the feeling of parting forever, which she often had, because when her family left a place they didn't often go back. She looked off toward the shops in the distance. This certainly is a pretty place, she thought.

"My wart!" she exclaimed. "I forgot all about it!" She looked at her hand and examined her finger. The wart was gone! She ran her finger over the place. It had really disappeared. She ran as quickly as she could to tell her parents.

She almost ran into Simeon Harrison, who was coming out of the old road.

"Mr. Harrison," said Emily, "you didn't remember me."

He stopped. "What should I have remembered?"

"That I talked to you this morning. I want to ask you something now. May I?"

"I remember you now. The girl with so many questions." He resumed his walk, turning in the direction of his house.

She walked along beside him. "Why do you go away so much and for such a long time when it's so beautiful here?"

He looked at her in surprise. "Is that what you wanted to ask me?"

"No, but I wondered."

"Well, the whole world is very inviting. Each place is attractive in a different way."

"No," she disagreed, "all of it isn't. An awful lot of it looks the same to me — except here, of course, and a few wonderful places hard to get to, like the Smoky Mountains or places in Maine or like Yellowstone Park, which we are going to see some day."

"So you've seen most of it — most of the world?" Mr. Harrison asked.

She nodded.

"What would you say the world looks like?"

"Long white roads rushing toward you. . . . Places to eat near gas stations, motels. . . . Every once in a while you come to a town, but it's usually like the town you just left."

"You don't seem to enjoy living in a trailer."

"It's a motor home," she corrected him, "and I do enjoy it. I enjoy mountains and trees and lakes and rivers, but there are not enough of them compared with the rest, and you can't always stop, you know. I like an old place like St. Augustine. And the ocean! Every time I go to the ocean I almost like it best. But there is only one Green Circle!"

"And what is a 'green circle'?"

"Oh, that's the name of the place where I am now, down by the river. That's what I call it. It's really your land, but sometimes I pretend that it's ours. I've always hoped that we could have a little land, and my father has, too. He said we'd know it when we saw it, and we did! The minute I woke up in the morning, I knew! I knew! It was the promised land. It was then that I named it the Green Circle."

Simeon Harrison did not answer at first. "What is your name again?" he asked.

"Emily Crump. You were just talking to my mother and father. I'm their daughter."

"Ah, yes. And you like it here?"

"I do. I always wanted to live near water."

He laughed at that. "That river isn't a very important one. It is only a branch."

"It's just right for me. I think it's beautiful," Emily said.

"It might be at that. I gather you don't like to travel all the time?"

"No, my father and I want to settle down. My mother is the get-up-and-go one, but even she likes this spot. Mr. Harrison, couldn't we stay here a little while?"

"Stay on my land? And what would I get out of it?" He spoke with sarcasm.

"Friends near you, of course . . . to help you if you get sick or anything. And money. We'd pay, of course. We always pay."

"I'm relieved to hear it." He gave a sigh. "No,

Emily, you're a very nice child, and I like you, which surprises me, but I'm afraid there is nothing I can do. I can't make exceptions."

They had walked to the front gate of Harrison's home.

"Well, good-night," said Emily. She turned away.

"I'd like to oblige you," he said again, "but I just can't have squatters on my land."

She faced him again. "What are they? I'm sure we're not — what you just said."

"Well, trespassers, then. Do you know that word?"

"Yes. It's all right, Mr. Harrison. I asked too much."

"Good-night," said Mr. Harrison. "I guess I won't see you again. I've just told your parents they would have to go as soon as possible. Your father said you would be getting an early start tomorrow morning."

"Tomorrow? We're leaving tomorrow?" Emily's heart fell. "But what if the new part hasn't come? The man from the garage said he wasn't really sure. Maybe we can't move tomorrow."

"Then I'd have to have your trailer towed away."

"Where would you tow us to?" asked Emily. She felt tears spring to her eyes.

"What does it matter? To the dump, I suppose. Let's cross that bridge when we come to it! Your father thinks you'll be ready to go."

"Tomorrow!" Emily repeated. She turned and ran away quickly, for she didn't want him to see that she was crying.

10
A Body in the Road

It was very early the next morning. Emily was on her way to the village to buy a few things for her mother. She walked slowly. By the time she reached the village, the shops would be open.

Emily was feeling sad because today they would have to leave the Green Circle. She had nearly reached the village when she saw someone lying in the road not far ahead.

If she had not been dawdling and dreaming, she would have seen the person sooner. It was a boy, somewhat older than Emily, tall and thin. He wore blue slacks, a T-shirt, and sandals. He was lying on his side so that Emily could not see his face very easily; his light brown hair was rather long.

She wondered if he was dead. He was very still. Perhaps a car had hit him and hadn't stopped. Why was he lying so still if he was not dead?

She knelt down and looked at him closely. How did people tell if a person was dead? Why, of course, if you were dead your heart stopped beating. He was lying on his side. Emily tried to reach his chest, but she had to turn his shoulder a little. His head fell back. He was very pale. He looked dead all right.

Emily put her hand on his chest timidly. She couldn't feel anything. She pressed her hand more firmly. Surely there was a faint movement. He was alive!

Desperately, Emily looked up and down the road. Where could she go for help? Even if she ran to the nearest house, how could she know if anyone would be at home? Perhaps she could wake the boy up. "Boy," she said, "boy, wake up! You are lying in the road." She shook him gently. There was no response.

She had to get the boy out of the road before she went for help. She had heard that in an accident you are not supposed to move an injured person. Well, she couldn't leave this boy where he was! She must try to get him onto the grass at the side of the road. Carefully, she turned him on his back.

Emily put her hands under the boy's arms and pulled him gently and slowly out of the road. With a final tug she rolled him over into the tall grass where he was out of danger. She saw a knapsack lying not far away and put it near him.

"Boy," said Emily, "can't you hear me? Please open your eyes. I want to help you. I'm going now to find a doctor — or a policeman. Please just open your eyes." But the eyes remained closed.

Now that the boy was safely out of the road, Emily ran as fast as she could until she came to a house. There was a little lawn and some purple flowers growing on a vine clinging to the side of the house, but there was no sign of life. She rang the bell and knocked loudly. There was no answer. Emily turned and ran the rest of the way to town.

As she went she wondered what she should do. Her father had told her when she was in any trouble to go to the police or a doctor or a minister. Then she thought that it was a doctor that was most needed, but how was she going to find one quickly? She would ask in the shops.

Almost out of breath, she staggered into the

open door of the bakery. There was no one there. She knocked on the counter, then on the top of the glass case, with its pans of fresh rolls and bread. There was the delicious warm smell of baking in the air as a girl of about sixteen came from the back with a pan of fragrant cinnamon buns just out of the oven.

"Please," said Emily the minute she saw her, "where can I find a doctor?"

The girl put the buns into a glass case. "What do you want a doctor for?"

"Someone is hurt. Please. I'm in a hurry."

"Well, he lives about two blocks that-a-way." The girl pointed over her shoulder.

"Could you tell me exactly how to go?" Emily asked. "I am a stranger here."

"Oh, where do you come from?" asked the girl.

"Please, the doctor! Which way do I go?"

"Go straight along in front here to the next corner, turn, and walk along the left side of the path until you come to his house."

"How will I know which it is?"

"There's a sign on it. Dr. Lane. It's a little yellow house. Who's sick?"

Emily rushed out. "I can't talk now," she

called over her shoulder. Her way was blocked by a friendly looking man opening up his shop.

"What's your hurry?" he said, stepping from side to side.

"I'm looking for a doctor," gasped Emily. "Please let me pass." She dodged around him. He said something to her, but Emily was already halfway down the block. As she dashed around the corner, she almost ran into a woman coming from the other direction. The woman grabbed her by the shoulders. "Here, here, child, not so fast. Where are your manners?"

"I'm going for the doctor. Someone has been run over, I think."

"You *think*? Well, the doctor has already started on his rounds. You see that old black automobile down there on the other side of the street? Well, the man coming out of that house is the doctor."

"Thank you!" Emily said, and sped down the street.

The doctor had his hand on the gate when she reached him. "Please!" She was breathing hard and couldn't speak for a minute. She was face to face with the bearded man!

"Oh, I'm sorry," she said, "I was looking for the doctor."

"I am the doctor. Take your time," he said, "take your time, little girl. Is someone ill?"

She nodded. "Down the road. It's a boy — I think he was run over!"

"Well, let's go," said the doctor. "Get in the car. You can tell me about it as we go along."

Emily scrambled into the front seat, and the doctor was at the wheel a second later. As he drove, he questioned Emily. She told him how she had found the boy and pulled him to the side of the road.

Even as she was talking, her mind was turning over everything she had thought about the bearded man. The answer to Grace Pertible's riddle was "doctor." She should have guessed it.

Dr. Lane parked the car across from the boy, grabbed his black bag, and knelt on the grass. He felt the boy all over lightly and gently.

"No broken bones," he said. He took a bottle from his bag and held it to the boy's nose. The boy's head moved, and he gave a slight snort and opened his eyes. Emily saw they were deep gray eyes set in long dark lashes. The boy looked up at Dr. Lane in a bewildered way but did not move.

"You'll be all right," said Dr. Lane. "Don't worry."

The doctor poured a little liquid into a glass. "Drink this," he said. The boy obeyed. After a minute he tried to sit up. The doctor helped him and supported him against his knee.

"What happened?" asked the boy.

"That's what we want you to tell us. Was it a car? Did you fall out? Were you knocked down?"

"I . . . guess so. I seem to remember something going by very fast. Then I don't remember anything else. I was walking. I came to see Mr. Simeon Harrison . . . but I couldn't find him."

"Well, that narrows things down a bit. What's your name?"

"Mark. Mark Hoban."

"Where do you come from?"

"Just a little place. You wouldn't have heard of it," the boy said. "Thank you for helping me." He tried to get up.

"That's all right. Do you think you can stand up?" The boy nodded, and the doctor helped him to his feet. Mark swayed. "I guess I'm dizzy," he said, with a weak smile.

"That's all right. You just have to get into the car. Did you have any breakfast?"

Mark shook his head.

"When did you eat last?"

"A long time ago," said Mark. "Day before yesterday — "

"I thought so."

Mark looked at Emily. "Is this your daughter?"

"No, this young lady told me you were hurt. I'm a doctor."

Emily liked the look in Mark's eyes. If I had a brother, she thought, he would be like this — just this age and everything.

"*You* found me?" Mark asked. "Thanks."

"It was nothing," said Emily, embarrassed. "I mean — it's okay."

Dr. Lane took Mark's arm and put him into the front seat of the car. "Hop in, child," he said to Emily. "I'll take you home."

Emily hesitated. She knew that she should go on to the store, but how could she leave before she knew how this would end? She got in the car. She hoped her parents wouldn't worry. She began to think of how she would explain.

The doctor drove to the Harrison house. "This is where Simeon Harrison lives."

The boy's face lit up. "Honest? Good grief! What d'you know?"

"Does he expect you?" the doctor asked.

"Well, no, I've never met him," said Mark.

"I did write a letter once, but he may not have received it."

"Well, I'd better go in and speak to him first." Dr. Lane went up the walk and rang the bell.

Mr. Harrison came to the door. "Oh, George, hello. Good to see you. What brings you here at this unholy hour? Come in, I'm just having coffee."

"I've a visitor for you, Simeon," said Dr. Lane. "That boy in my car."

"For *me*?" Mr. Harrison looked over the doctor's shoulder and stared at Mark. "I never saw him before in my life."

"Well, he said he was on his way to see you. He had an accident. I think a car knocked him down just down the road a piece. He's still a bit dazed. I doubt he's eaten for some time, and he must have food right away — light food at first, and he should be put to bed. He'll be all right in a little while. I'll bring him in."

"Hold on!" said Mr. Harrison, sounding annoyed. "Are you proposing that I take him in? I can't have him saddled on me!" A stormy look came into his face. "Just take him away with you."

"Well, he came to see you," said Dr. Lane.

"That's what you get for being famous. Nice-looking lad. Oh, and Simeon, he may be a runaway. Find out if you can where he lives so we can contact his home."

"Leave me out of it," Mr. Harrison said. "I'll have nothing to do with it. I'm busy." He looked at Dr. Lane, who was smiling.

"I'll take him a cup of this coffee," said Dr. Lane, pouring a cup.

"Help yourself," said Mr. Harrison. "Well, I'll go speak to the boy, but that's all." He bounded down the walk. "Hi!" he said to Mark.

Mark's face flushed. "Hi!" he said. "Mr. Harrison, this is great. I'd know you anywhere."

"Oh, you would? Have we met before?"

"Not exactly. But I've read things you've written — I've seen you on television. I wrote to you once."

"Drink this," said Dr. Lane, giving him the coffee.

"What's your name?" said Mr. Harrison.

"Mark Hoban. I'd like the chance to talk to you about something."

"I begin to see," said Mr. Harrison. "Well, fire away."

Mark looked at Dr. Lane, who was standing

beside the explorer, and glanced at Emily, who was leaning forward in the backseat. "It's private."

"Now's your chance," Mr. Harrison said. "No time like the present. What's it about?"

Mark drank some coffee.

"Well, I want to be an explorer," he said. "It's really about something you said last month on television — about climbing Nanga Parbat, the next mission you make. . . ."

Mr. Harrison looked pleased. "Yes, what about it?"

"Where is that — Nanga Parbat?" asked Dr. Lane.

"It's in India. It's the second highest mountain in the world," Mark answered. Then he said shyly to Mr. Harrison, "I came to ask if I could go with you."

"Absurd!" Mr. Harrison stared at him. "You surprise me! How old are you?"

"Nearly fifteen, and I've been climbing a lot. In the White Mountains. Other places, too. I'm good at it. One of my grandmothers lives in Denver, and I've climbed a little in the Rockies. But I didn't get to the top."

"One doesn't always get to the top!" said Mr. Harrison dryly.

"Now, see here, Simeon," said Dr. Lane, handing him Mark's empty coffee cup. "Mark has had a tough experience. He got off lightly, but he needs something to eat right away, and he must rest. No more talking for a while. Have him take a shower first — get some of that dust off. Then a nap and food — whichever comes first."

"Absolutely impossible!" said Mr. Harrison. "If I did things like that, I'd never have any privacy, never write a book, never get an expedition planned. Every mail would bring a letter, every car would stop at my gate. This is not my responsibility."

He shrugged and turned away. Then he turned back. "Mark — is that your name? You must understand — it takes years of serious preparation, serious study, special training — just think about that."

Mark did not answer. His face was red, and he stared in front of him.

Mr. Harrison went into his house and the door closed behind him.

"Sorry, son," said Dr. Lane. "I'll take you home with me, after I drop Emily off."

"I'm almost home," said Emily, slipping off the backseat and opening the door.

"You can let me off, too," said Mark. "I don't want to impose on you. I'll be all right. Thank you, Doctor." It was an effort to speak. His voice was low. He kept his head down.

"Nonsense. You're my patient now. Happy to have you. Will you be all right, Emily?"

"Yes, thank you, Doctor. It's just a little way. We're down that roadway. We're in a motor home."

"A motor home! That's terrific." Mark was recovering his voice.

"I guessed you were one of those in the motor home," Dr. Lane said to Emily. "I saw you coming in the other night."

"We saw you, too," said Emily.

"You looked as though you might be in trouble. I rode along behind you, in case you needed help. Then I saw you turn off into Harrison's lane. I thought you'd be all right, so I went home."

"It was awfully late," said Emily.

"Sure you'll get home all right?"

"Sure. Good-bye. Good-bye, Mark. See you."

"See you," said Mark.

Emily ran along the old dirt roadway, thinking about Mr. Harrison. How different he seemed now from the man she had talked to in the garden. She saw that he would never let them stay, even for a little while. People were just annoyances to him.

"That's all we are — annoyances." She repeated the word as she went along.

Annoyances, annoyances. . . .

11
Emily Runs Headlong into Trouble

Emily's parents were waiting under the awning.

"Guess what?" Emily called, as soon as she was near enough to be heard.

"Tell us. I can't possibly guess," said her mother.

Emily took the last few steps, and her mother kissed her.

"I've met the man with the beard," said Emily. "He's a doctor!"

"You haven't been in an accident?" asked her mother in alarm.

"No, but there was an accident. A boy was lying in the road. He was run over and I found him." Emily was beginning to enjoy the attention.

"His face was white and his eyes were shut, and I pulled him off the road and ran to get help. I found the doctor — and he was the man with the pointed beard!"

"Are you sure it's the same man?" asked her father.

"Yes, yes, of course. His name is Dr. Lane, and he was following us because he wanted to help us. He told me! He's very nice. And the boy's name is Mark something, and he wants to be an explorer."

"Well, you certainly had an adventure," said her mother.

"Mark was trying to see Mr. Harrison to get a job as an explorer, but Mr. Harrison wouldn't listen to him."

"Did you see Mr. Harrison?" her father said.

"Yes, we went to the front door. He didn't want Mark to come in, so the doctor took Mark home with him."

"Emily, something has happened here," said her mother. "The alternator did not come, but it may come tomorrow. We were just waiting to tell you before we went to ask Mr. Harrison if we could stay another day."

"We want him to know we're not trespassers," her father said. "And we thought that since you

101

want us to buy this acre, it seems a good time to make an offer for it."

"The way he acted today," Emily said, "I don't think there's much hope."

"We can only try," her mother added. "Since you and your father have fallen in love with this place, I'll go along."

"We'll be back in twenty minutes or so," Emily's father said. "Will you be all right?"

"Of course," said Emily. "May I just go and see the woods on the other side? There's a bridge down there, a little flat bridge. It's not far."

Her father stopped. "I noticed it. I'll go with you early tomorrow. Be patient. We'll find the time to explore before we leave."

"I could go by myself," said Emily.

"Woods are hazardous. Better not."

"I could go in just a little way," Emily insisted.

"I'd rather you didn't," her father said. "You never know what you might run into. You might get lost."

Emily laughed. "I'll leave a trail of bread crumbs like the Babes in the Woods."

"The birds ate the crumbs, remember?"

"Oh, well, I'll let out a thread as I go, like the Greek man in the maze with the Minotaur."

"We'll talk about it later," her father said. "It

looks like rain. You stay here and read your books. Your mother and I will be back before long."

Emily watched her parents go. Then she looked across the water. If they were leaving the next day, when would she have another chance to see the woods? The oaks that spread over an undergrowth of palmettos were old and huge, perhaps hundreds of years old. They were hung with mysterious streamers of gray moss. There were tall pines, too, and vines with small yellow trumpet flowers. All was still and peaceful. How could anything there harm her?

She thought that she might at least walk down to the bridge if she stayed on this side of the river. As she went, she thought over what her father had said. She decided that he had not *forbidden* her to go into the woods. What were his exact words? "I'd *rather* you didn't." That was almost a permission to decide for herself.

Emily reached the bridge, a flat wooden structure leading to an overgrown path on the other side. There seemed to be no road there, just a continuation of the path on this side that probably led back to the Harrison house.

The path on the other side of the bridge disappeared into the woods. She thought she would just walk over the bridge about halfway. There was a railing, and she rested her hands on it and looked up and down the river. How beautiful everything was! She was at the end of the bridge almost without noticing, so she thought she would walk a little way along the path. Surely that would be all right.

But once her feet were on the other side, they took her along to the edge of the woods. The woods looked different here. There were tall huckleberry bushes covered with waxen bell-shaped flowers like tiny snowdrops. There were vines of yellow jasmine. There were violets everywhere. She would gather a few of the lovely yellow flowers and a few pale violets to put in Grandma Wigglesworth's crystal vase. Then she would go right back. She would tell her father and mother how it had happened as soon as they came home.

The trees seemed to beckon her.

"Good-bye," she said. "I am soon to leave you!" She made quite a big bunch of the violets, wandering farther and farther under the trees where the ground was covered with pine needles and fallen leaves.

When Emily turned to go home, she didn't see the path. Surely she had passed that big oak over there? She went that way, but the path was not just beyond the tree as she had thought. She stopped and looked around. Every direction seemed the same. Her breath came in short gasps. She wondered if she were lost. She tried to laugh, saying she forgot the bread crumbs, but she was frightened.

Were there any wild animals? Someone had said that there were black bears in the Florida woods, but surely they were gone long ago. She had been warned about snakes. She knew that she must always look where she was going. Her father had said that you must walk in the woods with authority, so that you shook the ground a little and the snake could get out of the way. "The poor thing is more afraid of you than you are of it," he had told her. "If you see one, or hear a rattle, make no sudden move, but back off slowly, very slowly."

It was getting darker. That was curious, for it was still early in the day. A mist was curling through the woods. It began to look too heavy to be mist, and there was an acrid smell in the air. What could it be? She sniffed. It was the smell of burning!

Emily heard sharp, crackling sounds coming from the left. Then as she turned she saw the red

flames climbing up the trunks of the pines in the distance, and she knew that the woods were on fire. A little wind was blowing the flames nearer. She must not go that way — but what if it were the way home?

She began to run. "Don't panic, don't panic," she said aloud. A large bird flapped through the trees. She looked back. Black smoke billowed up over a tall sycamore in the path of the lurid glow. The fire was still quite far away. It leaped up a dead tree, making a torch of it. She knew she must run away from it, even if she headed in the wrong direction.

There was a wooden house in a clearing ahead and she raced toward it. A wild-looking woman and a man were putting wet blankets on the roof. The woman was drawing water from a well, soaking the blankets, and handing them up to him. As soon as she saw Emily the woman screamed, "Go away! Go away! Don't come here! Go on! Go on!"

Emily leaned against the fence to catch her breath. "Which way is the village? I'm lost."

"Don't go back! Go west — that way." She pointed. "Go as fast as you can."

"Let me stay with you. I'll help."

"No, no. We can't be responsible for you." The woman was wild and frightening. The man gestured Emily away.

The palmettos and thorns tore her jeans and scratched her legs as she crashed desperately through the underbrush. There were briars, too, some laden with blackberries. She had to go around them. She was afraid she might lose her way.

Her parents would look for her, she told herself. But suddenly she realized that the woods were the last place they would look. They had trusted her to obey them, but she had done the very thing she had been told not to do.

Emily looked behind again. The fire was sweeping nearer. There was a sheet of orange-colored light against the sky. The underbrush was blazing, and little rivulets of flame were running over the pine needles.

Emily stumbled. She said the prayer she knew best. She wondered if flames could leap the river. What if the *Venturer* burned up? It was their home. She should have been there to give the warning. She ran and ran. Without being aware of it, she had dropped the flowers she had picked.

What path was she on now? It wasn't the one she had first found, but it might take her out of the woods. The path seemed to open up before her as she ran. Something seemed to be leading her. She moved faster now than she had ever done in her life. She came to a wide path and, a few yards away, she saw the bridge.

There was fire now at her right so that she could see it as she ran. It was gaining on her. It was roaring through the pine trees. As she dashed across the bridge, a big turtle slid into the creek with a splash.

In a few minutes, she was back at the *Venturer*. She looked in the door. Her mother and father had not come back.

Emily leaned against the doorpost, and her breath pounded in her throat. A great wave of thankfulness for her escape swept over her. But she must find her parents and Mr. Harrison. It was his land. He would know what to do.

12
FIRE!

Emily ran through the grove along the back path to the Harrison house, and as she neared the house she called with all her might, "Mr. Harrison, help! It's fire. FIRE!"

Emily saw her mother and father. "Oh, come quick! There's a fire in the woods. The whole world is burning!" She leaned against her father, gasping for breath.

"How near is it to us?" asked her mother.

"You can see the flames across the water from the *Venturer*."

"I'll alert the village and call Bruce. He'll get the neighbors," said Mr. Harrison. "We have a volunteer fire unit, but no equipment." He dashed off to telephone.

"I'll go and see what I can do," Emily's father called after him. "Elvira, keep out of danger. Hang on to Emily." His voice trailed back to them as he sped along the back path. They ran after him.

Even before they reached the *Venturer*, the sound was terrible; the stench strong and unpleasant. The fire had burned almost to the opposite bank of the river, but was still about two hundred feet from the bridge. It was across the water, but coming nearer. Flames were licking the trees beyond.

Mr. Harrison ran up carrying several shovels. "We must dig trenches to slow it down," he said, as Emily's father grabbed a shovel. "First, we had better protect your trailer. Saturate the top so that no flying sparks can catch there."

"It's supposed to be fireproof," said Emily's father. "Let's try to stop the fire first. It may rain. I hope rain comes in time!"

"Don't count on it!" said Mr. Harrison. He started toward the bridge with Emily's father close behind. "Those clouds may not even bring rain at all."

About twenty feet beyond the Green Circle, the two men began to dig a trench, throwing the dirt up along it. The gardener, Bruce, and some other men had appeared in the woods on the other side where the bridge was in danger. They were beating back the blaze with blankets and small rugs. Emily could see the flickering lights crawling through the dry grasses. Three men were digging a long ditch.

Several more people now came running down the road. They carried buckets, rugs, shovels, blankets, and brooms and dumped them all in a heap until they should be needed. A bell was tolling in the village to give the alarm.

Emily's mother rushed into the kitchen and took down the largest bath towels from the linen shelf. "There's all that flowing water, useless," she mourned. "Bring the bucket," she said to Emily, at her heels.

The volunteers were following Mr. Harrison, each carrying something. Emily and her mother joined them. There was a sudden shout of dismay, and all looked down the river. The bridge was on fire. The planks were burning on the far edge, and bright moving lights were running along the railings. Three men on the other side were already trying to smother the flames.

Emily's father and Mr. Harrison flung down their shovels and rushed toward the bridge to help. Others began to soak blankets at the water's edge and to hand them up to the fire fighters. The men tore the railings off with the wet blankets and dropped the burning wood into the river.

Soon the fire on the bridge was out. There were charred holes at the end, and it had lost part of its railing, but the bridge seemed safe now. The fire had burned through the trees and bushes just behind, leaving blackened empty places, then roared away, pushed by the wind.

Dr. Lane came, bringing Mark. Without wasting an instant, they plunged into the fight. A number of volunteers went across the bridge to help those on the other side. Emily started to go with them, but her mother put a hand on her shoulder and held her back.

Just then, a bush that slanted over the path in front of them suddenly flared up, and a flaming branch fell across the space, setting fire to the grass around them.

There was a shower of sparks as it fell, and Emily's mother jerked Emily away and put out the sparks that had fallen in her hair. Other tall bushes near them ignited, and now the swift fire was on both banks, coming closer to the Harrison home and the *Venturer*, too.

Other people had come to help and were frantically digging trenches to halt the new danger.

Emily and her mother joined the others trying to beat out the flames with wet towels. Emily's father, Mr. Harrison, and several others were also attacking the flames as they came from the bridge. A wind was rising, but it seemed only to blow the flames nearer.

It was growing dark. The constantly changing and moving light of the fire was terrifying, and the heat almost unbearable. Emily and her mother soaked their towels, scooping up a bucket of water to use to wet them again, but the towels were soon useless. Someone tore a blanket and gave Emily half.

She never forgot the rhythm of that movement, as her arms rose and fell in time with the people on each side of her. She remembered, too, her sudden fear when the fire rushed past her along the ground, and she had to turn and try to stop it. It was like a living enemy — a *thing* determined upon her destruction. Her whole mind and body were bent upon one thing, to save the *Venturer*, and to keep the fire out of the Green Circle.

The fire seemed almost under control when it caught in a grove of six or seven evergreens on the opposite bank. It climbed up a huge pine at the very edge of the water, fifty or sixty feet high.

The fighters on the other side were powerless to stop the flames.

The great tree swayed and crashed with a hissing sound into the stream, pulling roots and soil from the bank. In a wild gust of wind, flames seemed to leap out through the air as the pine tree went down. Some flames fell onto a great limb of an old oak tree that stretched over the water. First some dead branches on the limb blazed, then leaves and dried moss.

Voices were murmuring, "What next?" and "Tough luck." A woman next to Emily said, "That beautiful weather we had was a curse. The trees and grass are as dry as tinder."

If the fire creeping along the oak limb reached them, it would bypass the trenches and bring the danger nearer to the *Venturer* and to Harrison's house, and after that to the houses down the road. Something had to be done — fast!

Emily saw Mark fling down his shovel and rush to the water. He dived in and swam like an Olympic champion out to the limb. Over his head, the flames were eating their way along the limb toward the bank.

Mark caught a strong branch sticking out from the limb. The motion sent small fiery branches falling from the end. "What's he doing?" Emily called. Mr. Harrison came up behind her.

"I know," he said. "He's going to try to bend the limb."

Mr. Harrison ripped his shoes off. "Be careful, you young idiot," he called, and then he, too, swam out. With Mark's help, Mr. Harrison was able to swing himself up on the oak limb. He sat astride it, and with a branch he broke from above his head, he pushed off the lighted moss into the water. Mark, quick to see what to do, was also pushing off the moss and splashing water on the limb with his free hand.

Mr. Harrison kept sliding down the limb, trying to make the end dip down into the river to put the fire out. With Mark pulling the limb from underneath, they were able to bring the burning end almost to the water. The burning moss slipped into the river, making a sound almost like the buzzing of a swarm of bees.

Using all their strength, the two managed to push the limb all the way down into the water at last. There was a sound like an angry snarl. Mark's eyebrows were singed and his face scorched and crimson from the heat and exertion as they gave one last effort and dipped the limb again. The flames went out.

Mr. Harrison slipped into the water. "Come on," he said, and Mark swam with him back to land. "That was well done," said Mr. Harrison.

"Will I make an explorer?" Mark asked, his breath short and painful.

"You might," said Mr. Harrison, climbing onto the bank. "But now there's more to do; we can't stop."

The fire continued to burn in other parts of the woods.

Suddenly there came a flash of lightning and a clap of thunder. Two big drops splashed in Emily's face. "I felt rain!" she exclaimed. Then heavy drops spattered all around. Storm clouds rolled overhead. With a burst, with a rush, a mighty downpour almost drenched them. A shout of joy went up as the rain poured down. Now the danger was over. The fire would soon be out. The people scattered and ran, most of them down the old driveway to the main road.

"You're a great little kid!" a man who had been working beside Emily called to her as he left. She found her mother, and together they ran for the shelter of the *Venturer*. They were almost soaked before they reached it. A woman said as she went by, "I live down the road — the yellow house. Let me know if I can do anything for you." Emily's mother could only smile and wave; the woman was already out of earshot.

Emily's mother lit the lamp. Emily looked at herself in the little mirror. Her brown hair was singed, her face was dirty, and her hands were so grimy she couldn't tell whether they were scorched or not. Her clothes were tattered and stained beyond repair.

"Come, dear, and put on something dry," said her mother.

She, too, was grimy and scorched. Her hair had come undone and hung loosely over one shoulder. Emily thought she looked beautiful even like that.

The door of the *Venturer* opened, and Emily's father came in with Mr. Harrison. Emily's mother handed them both big towels. "Mop yourselves off," she said. "We won't be long. I'll make some coffee. Make yourself at home, Mr. Harrison." She pulled the dividing curtain between them.

13
Emily Faces
the Consequences

Emily was already washing. Her mother gave her clean jeans and a T-shirt. Emily slid off her sopping sneakers, washed her feet hastily, and decided to go barefoot. She gathered up her soiled clothes.

"Put those things in the corner," her mother suggested, "and I'll deal with them later." With a clean dress over her arm, Emily's mother went into the shower room. The sound of the shower mingled with the sound of the rain beating on the roof.

Emily's father found dry clothes for himself and Mr. Harrison. They washed up at the sink and changed.

"Do you think all the danger is over?" Emily's father asked.

"Absolutely," Mr. Harrison said. "This is a real cloudburst. The woods will be soaked. Nothing more to fear from fire. But we did a great job while we had to. Thank you, Crump. I'd ask nothing better than you beside me in a crisis."

"It's very good of you to say so," said Emily's father. "By the way, what happened to that boy who helped put out the fire on the oak limb?"

"Oh, he's all right," said Mr. Harrison. "He went with Dr. Lane."

"He's a brave young man," said Emily's father. "And an excellent swimmer."

The two men watched from the windows as the downpour beat out the last vestige of fire, hit the trees and palmettos, washed the bushes. The flames retreated to a smoldering in the underbrush, and then expired. In a few moments the road was a flood, the space below the motor home a series of pools. The river was a torrent. Through it all the *Venturer* stood staunchly on its bit of high ground, sound as an ark.

Emily's mother came out as fresh as Sunday. She put a kettle on. Then she opened the door and stood looking out for a moment. There came a new smell — fresher, cooler, cleaner. Rain splashed on the sill. She closed the door. The kettle was purring. "Emily must have something hot," she said, "then I'll make coffee. Soup or cocoa, Emily?"

"Cocoa, please," said Emily in a small voice. She sat pale and quiet while her mother made the cocoa, buttered a slice of bread, and added some cheddar cheese. Her mother took out the beautiful blue and white china. She served Emily and made the coffee. Then she brought out the birthday cake. "You may have cake when you're ready, Emily," she said.

"No, thank you," Emily almost whispered. How was she going to tell them she had disobeyed them? The cocoa made her feel a little better. She drank it slowly.

Emily's father cut the cake for Mr. Harrison. Her mother poured the coffee, gave him some cream, and offered honey or sugar. "This *is* nice," murmured Simeon Harrison, putting in a teaspoon of honey. "I remember one time in the Indian jungle . . ." and he was launched on an exciting tale of tigers and elephants and hot coffee in royal tents. He paused in his story to say, "What delicious cake!"

He told them how he managed to get to places hard to reach, searched for things difficult to find, went into places that are hidden and secret and impossible for most people to see. Emily's thoughts were so loud, she hardly heard what he was saying.

Emily's mother poured more of the coffee that had been kept hot on the stove. "Best cake I ever tasted," said Mr. Harrison, as he began on his third piece.

The rain had stopped. "It will rain again," he said. "I'd better go home while I can. Thank you for all your help." He paused in the doorway. "If you leave before I'm up, and I don't see you again — it's been great knowing you," he said, and went into the darkness.

Emily sat quite still after he had gone. Her mother looked at her. "Poor child," she said. "You had a bad scare. You acted bravely, dear."

"Yes," her father said, "and with intelligence. What you did was absolutely right under the circumstances. Emily, I have to tell you — we did try to buy the land. But Harrison wouldn't sell."

"I was afraid he wouldn't," said Emily.

Emily's mother started to clear the table. "I'm so sorry," she said. "Get ready for bed, Emily, you need your sleep. You must be worn out."

"Oh, no! Not yet. I have to talk to you."

"Tomorrow," said her mother, putting away the table mats.

"No, wait." Emily had to tell them now. "You don't know the whole truth," she said. "I went across the bridge into the woods and I *did* get lost — then I saw the fire coming and I ran — and ran. I don't know how I ever found my way out."

Her father looked grave. "But you knew that I didn't want you to go into the woods alone."

"Yes, but I kept saying to myself, 'He only said he'd *rather* I didn't go,' but all the time I knew better. I'm sorry, Father — Mother. I feel just awful."

There was a silence. Emily wanted to cry, their faces were so sad. What would they do? She had made them unhappy. That was hardest to bear. She waited for them to speak, her heart thumping. Would they ever trust her again?

Finally, her father spoke. "Emily, unless you obey us, we can't protect you. But what's done is done. Sometimes, when a person realizes that he has been wrong, and sees that the wrong decision has an unhappy consequence, that can be very useful. Would you need anyone to remind you that when you went into strange woods alone, you were in danger of your life?"

"I'll never forget it," Emily said. "I wasn't brave. I was scared."

"Of course you feel awful, but be happy that when you saw the fire, you did what was exactly right."

Emily went to him and kissed his cheek. Then she kissed her mother. She was still their child. They loved her. They thought that she did some things well. Tomorrow she would work on the composition she had been putting off. And she would help her mother clean up. She would pack all her own things, too, instead of leaving it all to Mother.

Her mother put her arm tenderly around her. "You're a dear child," she said softly, "but sometimes willful."

"I plan to do better," said Emily. Then with a flash of laughter, "Another time, I'll at least take bread crumbs, or a spool of thread," she said.

14
Another Delay

The man from the garage came early the next morning. The alternator had arrived on the last bus the evening before, and he and his helper installed it. Emily and her mother sat together on the bench under the magnolia tree while the work was going on. Then Emily's father got into the driver's seat and turned the key. Nothing happened.

The man from the garage got in and tried. Still the *Venturer* would not start. "The battery's gone, I'm afraid," he said.

"Oh, no!" moaned Elvira.

"Looks like we're meant to stay," said Emily.

"Please, love, don't talk that way!" her mother said. "We're in danger of getting into big trouble. Mr. Harrison won't like it at all."

The men were pushing the motor home now; Emily didn't know whether they were trying to start the engine or put the *Venturer* back where it had been.

The terrible rains of the night before had soaked into the dry Florida soil. The world was radiant and green around them. Even the burned woods on the opposite bank showed signs of coming back to life.

The motor home had reached the place where it had been, and the men were jacking it up. Soon the mechanic was underneath.

"We must get word to Mr. Harrison," Emily's father said, "but I'd better stay here. Perhaps Emily could go? Would you do that for us, Emily? Tell him there's another delay. We're trying to find out what's wrong, and we'll leave as soon as possible."

"I wish he'd say that we could stay another week!" Emily said.

"Now, Emily," exclaimed her mother, "just give the message exactly as we've given it to you."

"I will. I promise." She ran off, going through

the little grove behind the Harrison house. She knocked timidly, and then more loudly, and Mr. Harrison came to the door in a dressing gown. He had been exhausted by the strain of the fire and had been deep in sleep. He was only half awake. "Are you still here?" he exclaimed.

"We've run into more trouble," explained Emily. She tried to repeat her father's words exactly.

"Why do you look like a kitten with a bowl of milk?" Mr. Harrison asked her. "Are you happy about it?"

"Well, yes," Emily said truthfully. "Because we can stay a little longer."

Mr. Harrison rubbed his face sleepily, trying to wake up. "I'll dress and be right there. Tell your father."

Emily stood looking at him for a minute, wishing that she could think of something to say. She wanted to know if he was angry.

"I'll come and see what I can do." The door closed.

Emily walked slowly back to the Green Circle. What would he do? If the *Venturer* wouldn't start, would he have them put in the hoosegow, as her mother said? She wondered what a hoosegow was like. Of course, she might find out very soon, if Mr. Harrison put them in it.

"He said he'll be here in a minute," Emily told her parents. She leaned against her mother, who put an arm around her.

Dr. Lane drove up in his old black car, with Mark beside him. "This is an unexpected pleasure," Emily's father said. Emily and her mother greeted them as they got out of the car.

"I've come to say good-bye," Mark said to Emily. "Dr. Lane says you may have saved my life. I'm catching the bus in the next town. I'm going home. Maybe I'll see you again sometime."

"I hope so," said Emily.

"I must go on and tend to a patient," said Dr. Lane. "I'll be back for you in plenty of time to take you to the bus stop, Mark." He stopped to speak again to Emily's mother.

Mark was curious about the flowing well in the field beyond. He looked at the way the stones were set to form a V-shaped channel. "It gives me an idea," he said. "It might work with a problem we have at home."

"Come and see my special rock," said Emily, and she led the way.

Mark looked around the Green Circle and said it was terrific. He saw where Emily's mother had put in the impatiens plants. They had pink blossoms and seemed to have already taken root.

"Mother has planted blue morning-glory seeds, but of course they come up later. She says you must always leave a place better than you found it."

"That's terrific," said Mark. "It might take some doing, though."

They sat on Emily's special rock, and she told him how much she wanted to stay.

"Maybe you will," said Mark. "Stranger things have happened. Maybe I'll see you when I come back. Because I'm not giving up. I'm going to be an explorer, and Harrison is the only explorer I've ever spoken to. I'm coming again to get him to tell me how to go about it. You and I will meet again, I'm sure of it!"

"If I'm here," said Emily. "If we're here. It is only a dream."

"Well, you can come back, can't you?"

"If my family wants to," said Emily.

"If you let me know where you are, I'll come and see you," Mark said.

"Would you?" said Emily, astonished.

"Of course, because you saved my life." Mark looked down at his feet. "I — er — have to keep in touch in case you ever need me to save yours. It's an obligation." He took an envelope from his pocket. "I'll write my address on this," he said. "Dr. Lane put his address in this envelope for me, but I can just tear off the flap. Oh, what shall I write with?"

"Father will have a pen." She scrambled up, and Mark did, too.

Just then Simeon Harrison came through the grove. He greeted the Crumps happily. "How are you, Mrs. Crump, after all the excitement yesterday? I'm still thinking of that marvelous cake." To Emily's father he said that he was not to worry too much about the delay. It gave him time to have the shirt he had borrowed laundered. He greeted the mechanic and his helper as if they were old friends and asked if there were anything he could do to help.

The mechanic crawled out from under the *Venturer*. He dusted his hands off and said he had to go back to the shop for something. "And to see if I have a battery that will do."

His helper was gathering up the tools scattered everywhere and removing the jacks from under the *Venturer*.

"I have some work to do. I'll look in again later to see how things are going," said Mr. Harrison. "Let me know if I can do anything to hurry things along." He started toward the path through the grove as the garage men drove off.

"I'm going to speak to him," Mark said to Emily. He straightened up and lifted his head. "It takes more courage than facing a grizzly bear," he said and went toward Harrison.

"Mr. Harrison, may I speak to you for a minute?"

"If you can be quick. I have some work I must do." He went to sit on the bench under the magnolia tree. Mark sat on the grass, and Emily beside him. Mark suddenly didn't know what to say.

"Well, fire away," said Mr. Harrison.

Mark found himself unable to speak. What could he say that he hadn't said yesterday? "It's just that I'm going home this afternoon, and I may not see you again. Mr. Harrison, I want to be an explorer!"

"I wonder if you know the dangers explorers face. Have you considered that an explorer must have twice as much courage as the ordinary person? And sound health, too."

"Of course I have," said Mark.

"Suppose you were in the Amazon jungle," Mr. Harrison went on. "An anaconda is slithering down a tree not far away. There are leopards in the woods. In your party there are three men. The leader does not get along with the others. You are running out of food and drinking water. You have to keep peace with the leader. Then there's that huge snake. An explorer must cope with this situation, or he doesn't come out alive. To quarrel with the leader is suicide. You can't run away. You must solve things where you are."

Mark was listening with wide-eyed attention. He didn't say anything.

"Are you sure you want to be an explorer?"

"I'm sure," said Mark. "But I'll keep out of jungles!"

"Mr. Harrison," said Emily, "what Mark wants to know is how he can go about getting to be an explorer."

"There's no magic way. He's very young. There are so many things he could be. An Olympic swimmer, for instance. He swims exceptionally well."

"But he wants to be an explorer," insisted Emily.

For the first time, Mr. Harrison smiled. "You have a lot of courage, Emily. Do you want to be an explorer, too?"

"No. I want to live in one place — a place like this. Go to school and have friends."

Mr. Harrison made a sound like a beginning of a laugh. "Well, you know your wish, anyway."

"What about Mark? How does he begin?"

Mr. Harrison frowned and didn't answer.

"It's all right, Mr. Harrison," Mark said. "I didn't mean to bother you."

"The first thing you must do, Mark, is to get an education."

"You mean college? Study things I may never use!"

"An explorer uses everything. Languages, history, science, geography certainly. Math. Art and travel, experience. Every summer, get a job connected in some way with the area you have decided on as your special interest. If you are serious, things will open up for you."

Dr. Lane drove up, and Mr. Harrison walked across the Green Circle to speak to him.

Mark went to say good-bye to the Crumps and held out his hand to Mr. Harrison. "Good-bye, Mr. Harrison. It was terrific to meet you."

"Good luck, Mark," said Mr. Harrison. "Get an education and come again and talk to me."

"Do you mean it? Will you remember me?"

"I'll remember you."

"You won't forget you said this?"

"I never forget what I say, for I never promise anything I don't mean."

Mark turned to Emily and said, "Don't forget me."

"Oh, your address!" Emily exclaimed. "Father, may we borrow your pen?"

Mark started to write on the envelope flap.

"Wait a second," said Mr. Harrison. "I have a notebook." He tore out a page. "An explorer always has a notebook," he said to Mark.

Mark used the hood of Dr. Lane's car for a desk, scribbled a few lines, and gave the paper to Emily.

"Come on, Mark," said Dr. Lane. "We mustn't miss the bus." Mark jumped into the car. "I'll see you soon again," said Dr. Lane to the Crumps, as they left.

"Good-bye," Mark called. "It was terrific knowing you."

15
Mr. Harrison Sees What He Must Do

Almost immediately, the mechanic drove up. Emily's father hurried over to him. The man didn't get out of the truck, but leaned over and spoke earnestly. Then he drove away.

Emily's father came over to Mr. Harrison. "The mechanic can't tell how long it will be before he can get another battery — there isn't one in the shop that will fit."

"This puts me in an awkward position," Mr. Harrison said. "It is well known that I don't allow anyone to use this land. It's a big help to have that reputation. On the other hand, I feel that I owe you something for your help yesterday. But if I let you stay any longer, how can I refuse other campers? I'd have a gypsy camp in no time!"

"That's not really so," Emily's father said mildly. "In my opinion, it's an absurd and defeating idea. Suppose a man asks me for a coin for a cup of coffee — someone obviously hungry or cold. But, no, I let him faint at my feet because if I give him anything, I'll have to give money to a hundred others who will immediately spring up and demand help. So the thing I should have done is never done, and I tell myself that it is beyond my powers."

"Edward believes in dealing with each thing on its own merits," Emily's mother said.

"Why can't you refuse other trailers and motor homes? It's your land," Emily's father said.

Mr. Harrison looked at him with interest. "You certainly have a point there, Crump," he said. "I don't know why I never thought of it that way before."

"I have an idea," said Emily's mother. "Is there a motel nearby where we could stay while we're waiting for the battery? We don't have to stay here if it really bothers you to have people on your land."

Emily couldn't bear the idea of leaving the Green Circle to stay in a strange motel. She drew in her breath sharply and turned and ran.

"Let me go speak to her, please," said Mr.

Harrison. "Perhaps I can think of something to say that will make it easier. And don't think about going off to a motel. I'm beginning to look like an ogre." He went across to Emily.

"May I sit down?" Mr. Harrison asked her.

"Of course. It's your bench," Emily answered. She made room for him and sat up stiffly. She did not look at him. She stared at the water.

No child should have a look like that on her face, thought Simeon Harrison. "Don't worry about going to a motel," he said. "You're going to stay right in your own home."

"Then will you have us towed away, like you said? I don't want to live in the dump!"

"Did I say that?" he asked in some confusion. "I didn't mean it. Do forgive me."

"Besides," Emily said, "I've been invited to go to school here, and I've been to school so *very* seldom!"

"We can't always have what we want," Mr. Harrison said. "You mustn't be unreasonable. Let's be quiet for a minute and try not to think. Listen to all that's going on around us. Don't even try to hear what I'm saying now — let it just be a voice murmuring, just as the water is murmuring in the stream. The water curls around the roots of that tree and passes the keystone rock. Did you know that white rock is coral and comes from under the sea? Florida is built on coral. Close your eyes and listen . . . listen . . . how many sounds can you hear?" He said nothing more.

Emily could hear a mockingbird in the wood. "Here, here, here," it said. The water gurgled as it went past. It seemed to make a different noise every time. A fish splashed. She opened her eyes, but not quickly enough to see the fish, so she closed them again. There was the "burr" of insects, a sound as of many little bells all ringing at once, far away. A car went by on the road, a distant rush. A whistle blew somewhere, a dog barked, and through all these faint sounds there was the sound of water rushing in the field. It had a strange odor, mingled with pine trees and the smell of the wet earth, and a heavy odor of burned grass.

"The water smells so strong and cold and funny," she said.

"That's the sulphur in it," Mr. Harrison told her. "What else do you smell?"

"The burned places in the woods," she answered, "but most of all the artesian well. Oh! And now something delicious. It's the magnolia, isn't it?" She opened her eyes and looked up at the great white magnolia blossoms, opening like pale lanterns in the large dark leaves of the tree that sheltered them, pouring out their rich fragrance.

"Now, look all around," said Simeon Harrison. "Tell me, what do you *see*?"

"I could see all this with my eyes closed," she told him, "I look at it so much. It's the Green Circle. Those purple flowers on the water — what are they called?"

"Hyacinths. We don't think much of them around here; they choke the stream. The yellow ones are mallows."

"They look like beaten biscuits, only prettier," Emily said. "We've planted some morning glories. Be sure to look at them when they come up. I'd love to see them open and then close again in the afternoon."

She looked at a shiny bug crawling along the ground. It was a small leather bug, polished and dark. A blue jay flew out of the woods, swooped in the air in front of her, and came to rest on the hedge. "I had no idea so many things were happening all at the same time," she said.

"I saw and heard a few things myself. When I was a little boy, my mother sometimes made me sit quietly and listen and smell and look at the world, and try to put all thoughts out of my head. It calmed me. I had rather a quick temper when I was a child."

"You still have," said Emily frankly.

He was startled. "I'm afraid I have, but I try to control it. I'm beginning to see that perhaps you're not as unreasonable as I imagined you were. When I look at the water and listen to the birds, see the yellow jasmine and magnolias, and those oleanders spilling out color — I must admit that if once you found this place and loved it, it would be hard to leave.

"I played here often when I was young," he went on. "My mother made this place. She knew about gardens. I used to swim in that river." He looked at Emily with sudden affection. "How old are you?"

"Going on ten."

He nodded. "Yes, I was just about your age. I'm much older now, but we could be friends, couldn't we?"

"Of course," she said eagerly. "All the Crumps will be your friends. I'll write to you if you like. When we had our eyes closed just now, I thought of something I wanted to tell you."

"You did? Tell me now."

She spoke carefully, trying to put her thoughts

into words. "If you have had something, and you remember it, in a way you always have it. I'll always have the Green Circle because I'll never forget it."

Mr. Harrison was moved by the generous light in Emily's eyes. The soft hair pushed back from her forehead had a red glow in the sunlight. She was just a slender little girl in blue jeans and a white shirt. Yet she had almost certainly saved Mark Hoban's life, and she had given the alarm for fire and may well have prevented it reaching his house and the houses on the road.

Mr. Harrison jumped to his feet. "Come with me," he said. "I must talk to your mother and father." He strode across the grass to where her mother and father were standing.

"Emily and I have had a talk," he said. "It reminded me that I have not been in this place on my land for some years, and so it is time for me to share it. You asked me yesterday to sell it to you, and I said under no circumstances. Well, I've just changed my mind. I've decided to accept your offer. I'll sell you this acre."

"Oh, Mr. Harrison!" Emily gasped.

"Do you mean it?" Emily's mother almost whispered.

He smiled, and they saw another and happier man. "I'd like you for neighbors."

"So we're agreed," Emily's father said.

"Agreed," said Mr. Harrison. He shook hands with Emily's father and mother and then with Emily. Her eyes were shining with happiness.

"The Green Circle is ours now," said Emily's mother.

Emily flung herself into her father's arms. Then she threw her arms around her mother. "Ours! Ours! Is it really true?" She looked up at her mother. "And, Mother, you won't mind staying here forever?"

"Well, I'll root here," she said. "But we'll keep the *Venturer* for the times when we have the urge to see something we never saw. And we'll have this lovely place to come back to."

"Maybe Grace and Jason could go with us to Yellowstone Park!" Emily's eyes shone with excitement.

"They certainly could," said her father.

Emily smiled at Mr. Harrison. "Thank you, thank you, Mr. Harrison. Now we are not only friends, but neighbors."